BEYOND A DISAPPOINTMENT

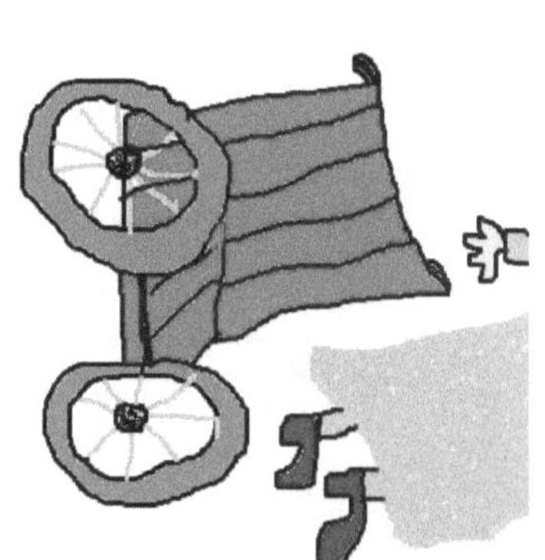

by

ISLEY ADAMS

Beyond A Disappointment

Copyright © 2023 by Isley Adams

ISBN 979-8-9875900-0-3

Printed in USA by Liberty Park Publishing LLC

*Kudos to those who forgive
and forget. Congrats to
those who push it down
and smile. Hello to the rest.
This book is for us.*

WEDNESDAY 2:55 P.M.

It was one of those situations we all describe as a worst-case scenario. Alone with a beautiful woman, not my wife, and she's asking for a ride home. Where's the worst-case part? It's located in the mud knocking at the gates of your denim backdoor. So what do you do? I'll tell you what you do. You clinch tighter, smile, and ask, "Which way you going?" That's what I did. What else would any soda drinking, Al-Qaida fearing American do? She told me to go west, so I did. I remember the CD in my deck that evening was some old R&B mix. Fit the mood perfect like.

Otis Redding sang as we drove and talked about safe issues. You know: weather, traffic, and how the city had changed over the years. I picked her up on her way out of spin class. I had seen her at the gym before. She was black. Dark skinned. She had large breasts and big brown eyes. I couldn't decide which I liked more. She asked if I was Puerto Rican, a common question. I told her I was mixed. My father was black, my mother white, and as a result, everyone thinks I'm Mexican. She laughed. I didn't.

As we turned left onto Marion Street, she had just about finished telling me her life story. Why do people do that? From what I remembered, she moved here about three years ago with her husband and two kids. The husband left, took one kid, she kept the other. He lived in New Jersey...or Minnesota ...or Hawaii- if not one of those, somewhere in between. The point was she's single, vulnerable, and lonely. Why couldn't she have just said that and saved me the torture of hearing her life story?

Her house was on the left side of the street between two homes with perfectly manicured lawns. I pulled over directly across the street from her house. She got out and said thank you for the ride. I said, "No problem," and asked if I could use her restroom. She hesitated, and then said, "Yeah, sure."

The inside of her house was bland. Besides the fact it smelled like a church, her house was nothing special. I was expecting something as stylish and sexy as she was. Nonetheless, I went into her bathroom, first door on the right.

Now using the bathroom at someone else's house is always a tricky situation. Do you 1: let it all out and stink up the place? 2: drop half the load and finish the job at your own house? Or 3: do the deed and tie up the bathroom for twenty-minutes and make sure no one smells what took place? Being a creative man, I chose to combine options 1 and 3. I'd stink up the place and try to cover it up, fail miserably at doing so, then exit her home hastily, leaving her to deal with the consequences of her kindness. I would not be getting laid. I ran the water to muffle the sounds of gas and repetitive flushing. "Is everything alright?" she asked.

"I'm good." I replied. After I finished drying my hands, I ran her toothbrush across my teeth a couple of times. Just a little keepsake.

"Thanks," I said, closing the door and the smell behind me. "You're a lifesaver." We exchanged a few more pleasantries before I left. I was in a hurry; I wanted to get out before that smell did. What happened next was a blur. I remember opening the door to leave and seeing a tall man walking toward me. Next thing I knew, I was in a head lock and she was screaming.

"Let go of his balls!"

"Not till he lets go of my head!" I said.

"Jesus Christ, Craig! Let go of his head!"

"Not till he let's go of my balls!" Craig said.

"Listen to her Craig; I've got a good grip." This went on for what seemed like an eternity before he finally let go of my head.

"That's a pussy way of fighting," he said to me while massaging his groin.

"Funny," I replied. "I'm not the one who gave up and let go first. I could have squeezed your balls all night, tough guy." Craig, I take it his name was, looked at me with a confused expression on his face.

"What are you, some type of fag or something?"

"Actually, I'm not. And if I was, I'd be a fag who didn't get my ass kicked." I smirked at him and straightened my jacket. I turned to the woman of the house and said, "Thank you again for your hospitality, sweetheart." She gave a half-hearted smile and said you're welcome. With what little pride I had left, I turned and headed out the door. Before I had gotten out of ear shot, I heard Craig ask her what smelled like shit. I laughed as I opened my car door and got in.

WEDNESDAY 4:04 P.M.

After stopping twice for fast food, I arrived home in a better mood. My wife, Rachel, was still at work. She worked at an insurance agency downtown. She was scheduled to get off at five, but I knew she wouldn't be home until at least nine o'clock. She was having an affair with her boss, Sean Gilbert. The problem with Rachel was she was too honest. She had told me about the affair a year ago. She felt that it was her duty, as my wife, to tell me of her infidelity. She also felt that it was her right to find true love, since our marriage was nothing more than a sham. You see, Rachel was not a native of the United States. I had purchased her online from a man in Vietnam for a little over eight thousand dollars. The website promised "true love" for the right price. Too bad all I got was one lights on pity lay a month, while her boss, Sean Gilbert, got the freaky Asian sex I so desperately paid over eight thousand dollars for. But you had to respect Rachel's honesty. Most spouses conduct their affairs in a shroud of secrecy behind closed doors. Not Rachel. She made color coded charts detailing where, and when her extramarital affairs would be taking place. She even had a column for dinner- very thorough charts.

I came inside the house and was greeted by my dog, Moose, an English Mastiff. He weighed over 150 pounds, drooled non-stop, and smelled worse the older he got. Moose was a lot like that old relative who comes to live his remaining years with you…except he didn't leave lights, stoves and radios on throughout the day. I petted his head and grabbed a beer from the fridge. We went to the living room and watched some talk show where the host was going to reveal who was the father of some uneducated, self-loathing, promiscuous, fifteen-year-old girl's baby- always good entertainment. I fell asleep after the third commercial break, or the third beer, I'm not sure which.

WEDNESDAY 4:57 P.M.

I awoke to the sound of Moose whining. He was scratching at the back door. After shaking the strange sensation that I truly missed something by falling asleep before the paternity test was revealed, I got up and let Moose in the backyard. I watched him sniff, spin, piss, and shit all in a matter of three minutes. I couldn't help but smile at the simplicity of Moose's life. He ate, slept, and loved unadulterated every day of his life. How many of us can say we do those things daily? Not as many as you might like to believe. I'm guessing it's somewhere around the same number of people who *honestly* buy *Playboy* for the articles. I continued to smile as I let him inside, but

I suddenly frowned when I realized that, if Moose were a person, he would have been the happiest person I knew. "He's not a person," I quickly reminded myself. But it was no use, I knew the point I was trying to make; and it was a good one. "Why can't I, or any other human for that matter, be as happy as my dog, Moose?" It was a simple, yet profound question.

Breaking my meditation was Rachel's car door slamming. I was surprised to see her home so early. She always parked on the street. I'd leave one side of the driveway open, but she never parked in it. Instead, she'd park on the street and walk to the house. I never understood why she did that. I never asked her either. I guess that would explain it still being a mystery to me after two years of marriage.

She came inside with a soft knock on the door. She always knocked when entering the house. Two years married and she still knocked when entering our home- cute. I assumed it was some sort of Vietnamese tradition. She placed her purse on the table beside the door. She laid her jacket on the back of a living room chair. I looked her up and down. Rachel had an exquisite knack of making unattractive clothes look sexy as hell. Today was no exception. She was wearing brown cowboy boots and a brown dress with orange polka-dots, circa 1955. On anybody else this outfit would look costume-ish. But on Rachel's 5ft 1, 112 lb. body, it looked like an alluring fetish. She topped the outfit off with shiny black hair and an orange beret. She reminded you of the woman you dated before you met your wife- sexy, intoxicating, and way out of your league. Moose started pawing at the door in hopes of seeing Rachel. I let him inside. Slobbering, he ran to her.

"Why you let him tack me? You know I hate slobber when Moose come."

"It's his way of saying he loves you," I said. "Besides, what does it matter? I assume you're only home to change clothes before heading over to Sean's house." She finished wiping the slobber from her dress before she spoke.

"You wrong. I stop home to give you message and change clothes for Sean house." I smiled at the near accuracy of my prediction. Minus one message, and a lot of broken English, I had correctly guessed her intentions. A small victory is still a victory, and that was all I was getting with her.

"Why don't you just take your clothes over to Sean's house," I said. "He's practically your husband anyway?"

"That what I come to message you," she said.

WEDNESDAY 9:49 P.M.

After a trip to "Lumpy's," the corner pub, a bar tab I seriously questioned, and an oddly introspective conversation with Toucan, the pub weirdo, I had boiled it down to this: Rachel was leaving me for Sean. She said he was a leader. He had the ability to inspire people. "He weads insurance company," she said, "you qwean up old people." I tried to convince her that caring for the elderly was just as exciting as being an insurance agent; it didn't work. The good news was she didn't want a divorce, she only wanted a separation. As a term of good will, she would still give me one lights on, pity lay a month. She felt she owed me that much. She was a fair woman. Toucan told me to respect Rachel's wishes and wish her luck in her new relationship. He said love and lust are two emotions all humans use improperly at times, so it's paramount to be understanding, for by God's grace, the scenario could easily be reversed. Needless to say, it really made me think. However, the profoundness in that advice was soon lost when Toucan then tried to convince me that sunlight carried sonic vibrations that could be bottled and reabsorbed when feeling depressed. I decided to discard most of Toucan's advice.

I left Lumpy's and headed home. I used the walk to clear my mind. The only problem was my house was too close. By the time I had gotten home, my mind was still cluttered with questions and curse words, so I kept walking. I walked on sidewalks, through backyards, and under bridges. Feeling a little more social, and a lot less drunk, I went into a convenience store. I grabbed a bottle of water and a bag of Skittles. The cashier mumbled something to me in Spanish.

"I'm not Mexican," I said. "No hablo Espanol."

"Oh, sorry. You look Hispanic," the cashier said. "I thought you…"

"No hablo English either," I said, putting my money on the counter. He gave me a confused stare along with my change. It was the kind of stare that questioned whether I was being serious, or whether I was being a dick. On my way out of the store, I glanced back at him; he was still trying to figure it out. I stopped walking, turned around and flipped him off. That should answer the question.

THURSDAY 12:34 A.M.

I slammed my unlocked front door behind me and sat in one of the living room chairs. I hardly ever locked my house doors. That used to drive Rachel mad. Rachel. Fucking Rachel! I couldn't believe her nerve! "I'm not a leader?" I thought to myself. "No one would follow me?" Fuck her! After all I had done for her. Hell, her name wasn't even Rachel for God's sake. It was Jiop Lin…. something. I never really knew her last name. It didn't matter. She was my wife, complete with my last name, moments after arriving in this country. I couldn't pronounce her real name, so I gave her the name of my ex-girlfriend, Rachel. The irony of the situation was that Rachel, the original Rachel, had also cheated on me. She dumped me for my roommate two days after Christmas my senior year of college. She said she wanted to start the New Year with a fresh slate. The humor in the similarities missed me at the moment. I was pissed. I kicked my shoes off and threw my feet on the coffee table. Moose was stretched across the couch. His tail wagged slowly, and he would look at me from time to time.

"You're not stressing over any of this are you, boy?" I said while rubbing his head. His tail wagged a little faster. "What am I gonna do, Moose?" While I sat there wondering whether I should ask Sean to pay me back the eight thousand dollars Rachel cost me, Moose rolled off the couch and headed to the back door. I again let him out and watched him sniff, spin, piss, and shit. Maybe it wasn't such a good idea to ask Sean for a refund. After all, wouldn't a refund void my agreed upon once-a-month pity lay? I knew I was mad, but not having sex with Rachel wasn't going to solve anything. It was obvious I needed to think this matter out more. I let Moose back in. He went and drank from his water bowl. If only my life were as simple as his, then I wouldn't have to worry about refunds for defective Asian brides, and how to continue having sex with them after they left you for another man. I wouldn't have to deal with people thinking I'm Mexican, or Puerto Rican, or whatever nationality struck their fancy. It would be so much simpler. No boyfriends putting me in headlocks for using their girlfriend's bathroom. No mortgage payment. No shitty job to go back to on Monday. Yeah, I thought to myself, Moose was the happiest person I knew. "He's not a person," I again reminded myself while walking to the fridge. But it was still no use, I knew the point I was trying to make; and it was still a good one. I grabbed a can of whipped cream and headed to bed.

THURSDAY 11:07 A.M.

A streak of sunlight woke me the following morning. I had taken my bedroom blinds down as an attempt at making a natural alarm. I asked myself, "What could be better than waking up to a rising sun every day?" Obviously, there's nothing better, so I took the blinds down and threw them away. I was aided in this decision by the apartment complex behind my house. The two-story apartment building was situated at the end of my back yard. The apartment positioned directly across from me was rented by a young, single lady. Her living room window and my bedroom window faced one another. I tried to make it a habit of giving her a glimpse of the goods. You know, changing clothes in front of the window, masturbating, things like that. Things women want to see men do but are afraid to admit. I think my goal was that she'd see my junk, try to fight the temptation, fail miserably, and finally come over to have some mediocre sex with a stranger. Simple enough, right? Every guy's dream. Not so much. What happened instead was she spray painted her windows black and lined them with aluminum foil. I, of course, took that to mean she was not interested in me sexually, and might have even been offended by my actions. I was both hurt and embarrassed beyond words. Luckily, as fate would have it, I didn't need to be. Turns out she was a meth addict attempting to hide from sunlight- that's all. I can't tell you how relieved I was to hear that.

I climbed out of bed, put on an ancient Oregon State tee shirt and headed to the kitchen. My brain was groggy from the whippets of whipped cream I took before going to sleep last night. Nothing makes you have better dreams than nitrous oxide, I thought to myself. Too bad I could never remember my dreams. I decided bacon and eggs would be my meal to start the day. I let Moose out to use the restroom before I started cooking. Now the secret to good eggs is a handful of cheese. Cheese makes everything better; that was my opinion. I finished buttering my toast, placed it on my plate, and headed for the couch. Moose was still outside. He could wait to come back in until I was finished with breakfast. I turned on the TV and started eating. Why is daytime television so terrible, I asked myself while flipping channels? Finding nothing that interested me, I turned the TV off and ate in silence. Crispy bacon was the best. I remembered a friend who actually liked his bacon soft and blubbery. He said that was the best way to taste the meat's actual flavor. A little too natural for my taste.

I finished my meal and let Moose back inside. Walking back to the kitchen I noticed the message light was blinking on my cell phone. The voicemail was from Rachel. She was calling to tell me she and Sean would be coming by after work to get the rest of her things. I didn't like Sean. And it wasn't because he was boning my wife. I mean that definitely contributed to it, but there were other reasons too. He was a small guy, about five foot six. He probably weighed 165 pounds or so. I just didn't dig his style. He wore gold necklaces and left the top two or three buttons open on his shirts. It looked sleazy. Plus he was Italian looking. I don't know if he actually was Italian or not, I just thought it sent a bad message. He looked like a stereotype. If I was Italian, I would kick his ass on principle. Luckily, I'm not Italian. Thank God. Those people give me the creeps.

THURSDAY 12:13 P.M.

Rachel would probably get to the house a little before or a little after five. That meant I had around six hours to decide if I was going to ask Sean for a Rachel refund, or if I was going to play it cool, or whatever other option crossed my mind. I needed to relax. I grabbed Moose and went for a walk. At first, I didn't know where I was going, but then it came to me- the skate park. I used to troll the skate park for barely legal skirt when it first opened a couple years ago. I never got any 16–19-year-old tail, instead, all I usually got was stoned. You know the drill, the kids notice me, notice I'm a little too old to be hanging at a skatepark, so a few approach and find out what the deal is. Am I a cop or a narc? No. Am I a pervert or a weirdo?

Yes, but hid very well. Do I mean any trouble? No. After that, they're pretty cool kids. They burn a few joints or pipe hits with you. They ask if you used to skate and what not, then they ask you to buy them beer. It's a time-honored tradition. Like splashing pedestrians on the side of a rain-soaked road. Or taking a picture of your genitals with someone else's camera. I was happy to buy them a couple forties of Old English, or Schlitz, or Milwaukee's Best. It was their money, so it was their gut-rot. Kids don't know, or care, what the hell they're drinking.

Moose and I made it to the skate park just as something big was happening. Everyone was circled around the bowl-shaped-thingy in the center of the park. Inside it were two kids going ridiculously fast and ridiculously high off jumps. The kids around me oohed and aahed and shouting out numbers and slang that I failed to grasp. Moose became excited and started knocking kids out of his way. I quickly realized that he weighed more than almost all the kids there, so I took him away for their safety. After things returned to normal, a lanky kid came my direction. He was shirtless, wearing a pair of cargo shorts and red shoes. His hair was shaggy and dirty looking.

"Got a lighter, bro?" he asked me.

"Sorry, I don't smoke cigarettes," I said.

"Don't smoke cigarettes, huh? Smoke anything else bro?" He laughed, obviously impressed with his innuendo. I laughed at how easy it was.

I passed the pipe around with them, off and on, for fifteen minutes. I decided it was time to leave when they started asking me to buy them beer. I told them normally I would, which was true, but I needed to get Moose home which was a lie. Strangely, I felt kind of bad lying to them. Moose didn't need to be taken home, truth was, I was ready to deal with Rachel and Sean. Maybe it was the fresh air, maybe it was the wacky tabacky, but it had finally become clear. Like any bad relationship, all you really have to do is step back and look at the big picture. Rachel didn't want to leave me. She wanted to be wanted. That's what it was. And Sean wasn't just some scrawny Italian looking guy boning my wife, he was an opportunist. All I needed to do was let Rachel know I appreciated her. Then, seeing how I understood her so well, she would come back to me and be the wife I paid over eight thousand dollars for. It was so simple. Sean was even easier. He'd probably walk away with his head hanging down after seeing Rachel run back into my arms. If he didn't, he might think about challenging me to a fight, but then change his mind after realizing he's giving up five inches and thirty pounds. I almost felt sorry for the guy; he was in over his head. I chuckled and glanced at Moose. He avoided eye contact for some reason.

THURSDAY 5:22 P.M.

Rachel and Sean showed up a little later than I expected. I made a point of folding her clothes and putting them in piles on the living room floor. I was trying to play along. She'd think I must not care about her leaving me if I took the time to fold and stack her clothes. But then I'd hit her with the emotional speech I'd been working on all day. She'd be so overcome with emotions, she'd run to me; kiss my face frantically and passionately (airport style), while Sean stood silently devastated with a pile of folded clothes in his arms. Basically, it'd be more dramatic this way. It might have been a little cruel, but it increased the odds of him walking away with his head down, thus decreasing the odds of me kicking his ass. It was really a win-win situation for everybody involved.

They parked on the street, probably by Rachel's instruction. She knocked lightly and entered. She was wearing a blue denim skirt with a yellow halter top. She had on yellow stretchy shoes. You know, the kind of shoes they give prisoners, or hospital patients, except yellow. Her hair was in pigtails. Again, this outfit would look a little trailer park on most, but she pulled it off. She always pulled it off.

Sean followed her in. He had on tight jeans with pre-made holes on the knees. His shirt, top three buttons unbuttoned, was a soft pink number, tightly tucked in behind a shiny black belt complete with a pistol shaped buckle. And as always, he wore a gold chain.

"What's up, dude?" he said as he entered.

I couldn't believe it. Two steps inside my door and he was already trying to test me. *"What's up, dude?"* I thought to myself. What are we, old frat buddies? He was officially on a short leash! I ignored his salutation. Rachel came and sat near me on the couch.

"Start taking clothes to car now," she ordered to Sean. He picked up a pile of clothes and said he'd be right back before leaving to the car. He left. I looked at Rachel. It was obvious she had something on her mind. It looked like

I had again guessed the situation correctly. She *was* bluffing about wanting to leave me, I knew it! She tried to speak, but I cut her off.

"I know what you're about to say," I told her. "You don't want to live with Sean. You don't want to leave me. All you want is for me to treat you the way he does. I haven't appreciated you or your honesty enough. I'm sorry. I promise I'm ready to make this marriage the marriage you dreamed about on the boat ride over from your country. I know you would have preferred a plane ride over, but like I told you before, it took my entire savings to buy you in the first place, so the boat was all I could afford. I'm still sorry about that, but the point is I want-" Sean came back and grabbed another pile of clothes. I stopped talking and watched him. He left with another stack of clothes. I looked back at Rachel. Her eyes. Her expression had changed, but there was definitely something on her mind.

"Listen," she said. "I not mad bout boat ride. I wike boat." She stood up and looked at a photo of us outside my parents' house. She walked back to the couch and sat down. Sean returned, grabbed another pile of clothes, and left. She reached out and placed her tiny hand on my knee. "You wong," she said. "I do want live with Sean. I wuv him. He leader and good to me. He have nice things. People fowow him."

I was shocked. "People fowow him?" I sat silently as she told me I was a nice man, that she still cared for me. I think she even gave me the "Don't worry, there's someone out there for you" line. I couldn't believe how American her break up speech was. Either women dumped men the same all around the world, or she had received a little help on the subject. It was the quintessential "dump a nice guy" speech. I was actually impressed until I heard her say something about the once-a-month pity lay.

"What? What about the once-a-month sex?" I asked, snapping back to reality.

"I no do it no more," she said.

"What?" I yelled in protest. "How the hell are you going to take that from me? You agreed to that, Rachel!"

"I think it make things compkated," she said.

"Compkated? You think it'll make things compkated? I'll tell you what'll make things comp-li-cated, Rachel; you losing your name! How do ya like that?" I shouted. She stood up and looked at me confused.

"What? I not know what you mean" she said.

"Your name, Rachel. I gave you that! You wanna give something to me and then take it back? Two can play that game," I smirked. "That's right- until I get my one day of sex back, you're no longer Rachel. It's back to Jiop Lin for you! Good luck with that." By this point I was standing with my arms crossed in front of me. I felt pretty good about myself.

"You can't take my name!" she said.

"Actually, Jiop, I think I can." She put her hands on her hips and gave me a nasty glare. We were silent for a moment which gave me time to survey the room and see Sean standing by the last stack of clothes. He looked at me out of the corner of his eyes and walked toward my wife.

"Is everything alright, Rachel?" he asked while rubbing her shoulders.

"Actually, Sean, it's Jiop Lin," I interrupted. "Is everything alright, Jiop Lin?" He stopped rubbing Rachel's shoulders and approached me. We were about four feet apart. His head was at my chest. I had a feeling he was going to do something he'd regret.

"I don't know what you two are arguing about," he said, "and it's really none of my business, but maybe we-"

"Maybe what, Sean?" I interrupted him. "Maybe you should stop talking little fella? Yeah. Maybe you should pick up Jiop Lin's last pile of shit. And maybe you should get the fuck out of my house. Maybe that, huh?" He tilted his head to one side and squinted his eyes at me.

"There's really no need for that kind of language, bro" he said while shrugging his shoulders. He walked closer to me and stared into my eyes. Forget the short leash; Sean had officially crossed the line. I stepped toward him. We were now a little less than two feet apart.

"You know what there's no need for, Sean?" I mockingly asked in a high-pitched voice, "five-foot three tough guys in my face." We were now bumping chests.

"I'm 5' 6" asshole!" he responded.

"Bullshit. You're carnival sized!"

"Stop it!" Rachel shouted. "You guys being dumb."

"Maybe you should listen to my future ex-wife, Sean. Because no matter how tall you say you are, you've got to be this tall to ride the ride," I said while tapping my chest about two inches above his head. "Wouldn't want you to get hurt." We stared at each other for a few more seconds as Rachel begged Sean to leave. Twice he flinched at me like a middle schooler in an attempt to frighten me. It was hard not to laugh at him. I knew I had him mentally broken. I stepped forward, bumping him backwards with my chest. I was thinking about hitting him when I heard a noise. It was a low growl. It was the kind of growl that made you stop and take notice. I became a little intimidated and hoped it didn't show on my face. I looked deep into Sean's eyes and saw it didn't matter, because his face showed the same intimidation. That's when I realized it was Moose growling. In all the years I had owned Moose, I had never heard him growl at anybody. I was pleasantly surprised to see him display his loyalty.

"Maybe you want to step outside," Sean said.

"I think that's a good idea," I replied, "unless you want your ass kicked by two people instead of one."

"Were you counting your dog?" Sean asked. "He's not a person, you know?" Of course I knew Moose wasn't a person, but don't you have artistic license when shit-talking?

We left Moose in the house and went into the front yard. Rachel repeatedly stepped in between us, and I called Sean a coward for hiding behind my woman. Seeing how angry this made him, made me happy. I kept it up. I was in mid-taunt when he swooped around Rachel, lunged, and took a swing at me. I pivoted to my left and started bouncing on the balls of my feet.

"So that's how you want it, huh, Sean? Cool. It's your funeral." I rushed him with a straight left punch that intentionally missed a little high. He ducked, naturally, to avoid the punch, and in doing so, lined himself up for a mean right hand. I hit him flush on the chin. He fell unconscious in my front lawn.

THURSDAY 9:29 P.M.

The crazy thing about a holding tank is this: no matter how few minorities live in your town, they're always the majority in a holding cell at the police station. There were six of us in there. Two were college aged white kids, probably in for driving under the influence or date raping some sorority girl. This was my best guess as I never had a chance to ask their offense. They nodded in and out of consciousness on the far corner wall. Besides them, there was one Mexican, two full-blacks and my half black ass. The two blacks claimed to have been detained on a case of mistaken identity. My black half believed them and shook my head in disgust at the racist judicial system. The old, "all black folks look alike, huh?" Figures. Meanwhile, my white half looked at the tattoos on their necks and told me to avoid eye contact. It was not uncommon for me to be torn on such matters. There's always two sides to a story, right? As for the Mexican, I had no idea why he was in there. I couldn't speak Spanish, and he couldn't speak English, so there was no use in even asking. However, I assumed it had something to do with someone's lawn care.

THURSDAY 11:11 P.M.

As an overweight deputy took me to get fingerprinted and photographed, I thought back on the evening's events. I wondered if hitting Sean was a good idea. From the outside I looked like a guy that beat up a man significantly smaller than me. Not a very sympathetic character. But I'd be a hero after they heard about the extenuating circumstances. Or at least a less repulsive bully. I didn't mind which.

"Do you have any relatives or friends we can notify to pick you up?" asked the chubby Deputy.

"Only one," I said. "The problem is, he's got four legs and can't drive without his head out the window." Failing to realize I was talking about my dog, or simply not seeing the humor, he placed me back in the holding cell. The two white kids were gone. I sat quietly on a bench and wondered why cops have no sense of humor. Maybe it was a prerequisite for the job? I also continued to analyze my fight with Sean. Why did I follow him outside? It was a good thing I didn't let Moose get a hold of him, or I'd be in even more trouble.

I smiled as I remembered the way Moose growled at Sean. I scrunched my eyebrows when I thought about what I had just told the chubby deputy. Moose really was my only family or friend. Now that Rachel had left me, he was all I had. That was sad. What was even more sad was the difference between our lives. Moose was happy, simple, and a pleasure to be around. I couldn't say the same for myself. I was miserable, jaded to an unhealthy degree and barely likable. We were complete opposites. I peed indoors. How could he enjoy being my dog? It was suddenly clear why Rachel had left me. What was I doing with my life? Where was I going? I couldn't say. That's why she liked Sean; he had answers to those questions. I had a depressing job at Harrington's retirement center. I bathed old people and dispensed pills. Where was the excitement in that? I needed a change. The first thing I had to do was become more like Moose- happier, easy going, and more of a pleasure to be around. Next, I needed to show Rachel that I was a leader, too. I had to prove that people would follow me. If I could do that, I could win her back. The question then became, how would I get people to follow my lead?

FRIDAY 7:02 A.M.

I watched the sunrise through my cell's tiny, barred window. It was the first dawn I had seen in a long, long time. Why does the sun look different then? I'm sure there's some scientific answer, but I didn't care. I didn't really want to know the answer. It was a stupid question. A better question was why hadn't I seen one in such a long time? I walked out of the county jail and headed for home determined to live more like Moose. That meant no more lying to people, no more cheating to get ahead, and no more looking up seated women's skirts, shorts, or dresses. Moose didn't do those things; therefore, I would no longer do those things. I was a Mooseologist? A Moosetian? I'd have to work out the terminology later.

There was a chill to the morning air. Kids walked to school with backpacks clung tight. Adults drove to work with coffee in hand. I smiled at the Rockwell scene and couldn't help but think something felt different. I felt like I was beginning some kind of a spiritual journey. I was a new man. I was also late to work. After walking home, letting Moose out, and showering, I was an hour behind schedule. I drove to Harrington's as fast and safely as possible.

Harrington's retirement center was a tan three story building. The third floor was what we called the "pen." It was where we kept the one-footers (one foot already in the grave). These were the seniors who were bedridden, completely senile, or viewed as a safety risk. Not a very pleasant floor to work on, and an awful place to live. The second story was filled with tweeners (not sick enough to move to the pen, but sick enough to need extra supervision). This floor was mostly filled with patients in the early stages of cancer, Alzheimer's or dementia. Oddly enough, this floor was a lot like its patients, not too bad. You could work or live on the second floor without too much complaint...for a while. The first floor was what we called the showroom. It was filled with our healthiest residents. It had a cafe. There was a community room where seniors gathered, danced, and watched movies. This was also the entrance to Harrington's Retirement Center. That way when middle aged men and women visited Harrington's, they saw a fun, lively place that made them feel less guilty about dumping their parents in an old folks' home. They had no idea what really went on inside Harrington's, and they didn't want to know. They wanted to believe their parents would be playing on the golf course during the day and living it up in the community room at night. And some did exactly that. But others didn't. And no one seemed to care too much either way. "Moose rule #1," I said to myself while looking for a parking spot, "don't dump your parents in an old folks' home."

FRIDAY 8:56 A.M.

I entered through the back door and scanned my timecard. I had a twelve-hour shift. On the bright side, nearly two of those twelve hours were already done. "Ten hours is nothing," I thought to myself as I put my backpack in my locker. When I closed the locker, I noticed Andy standing in the doorway. He was the guy I was supposed to relieve at 7 a.m.

"Where da hell you been?" he asked. "And don't give me no bullshit!" Andy was black, short, and country as hell. He moved here from Birmingham nine years ago, but still sounded like he just got off the bus. He was a happy man by nature. I apologized to Andy and even agreed to work the last hour of his next two shifts. I was trying to make up for my tardiness. He was a nice guy, Andy. A simple man. I always felt uneasy around him before today, and I'm not sure why. He wasn't the type of person to bad-mouth you or preach to you. He simply expected you to do what you're supposed to do. It was funny; he expected the same things Moose expected of people.

FRIDAY 12:15 P.M.

After more than three hours of pill dispensing, cafeteria clean up, and endless Bonanza episodes, I finally took my break. I usually spent my breaks in the staff lounge, or on the smokers' patio. I wasn't a smoker myself, but I found smokers to be less judgmental than nonsmokers- easier to talk too. That's part of the reason I spent my breaks with them. The other reason was being around smokers made me feel better about myself, like I was a better person. I mean seriously...smoking...it's a disgusting habit. I'd never seen Moose smoke. Good boy!

I sat down on a couch in the staff lounge and watched the news for a few minutes. Nothing in particular caught my attention. Some country was killing people in another country, a cop had been murdered locally, and an earthquake in Asia killed a mess of people. I must have missed the "feel good" stories of the newscast. What

I didn't miss was Mr. Rodriguez standing in the hallway. The staff was accustomed to Mr. Rodriguez wandering throughout the day. He liked to do a few laps around the second floor for exercise. He also had an eye for Mrs. Rodriguez (no relation) in room #214. I'd always catch him bringing her extra pudding cups late at night. You work in a retirement center long enough and you learn there's only one reason a man brings a woman pudding at 7:30 p.m.

Mr. Rodriguez was about 75 years-old, and in the early stages of dementia. The thing that made him unique was that he wasn't an ornery dementia patient. Most times, people become unpleasant when you tell them they're remembering things incorrectly. They get even more upset when they realize it's true. But Mr. Rodriguez was usually pleasant to deal with. He was a tall, lean old man. He had a slight tremor and a full head full of silver hair. I walked toward him and softly kicked his walker as a gesture of hello. He slowly turned his head in my direction.

"Hey, Mr. Rodriguez. Getting a little exercise?" I asked. He looked at me with familiarity in his eyes. I knew he didn't know my name, but whose name did he know? All he knew were faces and memories.

"Patricio?" he asked with a smile on his face.

"No, Mr. Rodriguez, my name's not Patricio."

"You're not Patricio?" He squinted as his head trembled. "I know you," he said.

"Yes, you do," I said, putting my hand on his shoulder, "but my name's not Patricio. In fact, I'm not even Hispanic, Mr. Rodriguez."

We walked a lap around the second floor together. Dementia patients are nice to talk your problems out with. They usually give great advice from personal experience, and they don't judge you because they forget everything you told them in a matter of hours, or even minutes. It's too bad a brain has to be damaged in order to behave in such a manner. However, I didn't do much talking that day. Instead, I listened to Mr. Rodriguez talk about his second wife, Erlina. He never mentioned his first wife. According to him, Erlina was the most beautiful woman to ever walk the earth. She had long black hair and beautiful breasts- a point Mr. Rodriguez emphasized more than once with big hand gestures. It was obvious he deeply missed her, and I enjoyed hearing him describe her. I was also impressed with Mr. Rodriguez's command of the English language. He didn't speak broken English. He sounded like a native speaker, only with a suave Spanish accent. It made him fun to speak with. I always imagined him as an old James Bond character. I guess that was part of the reason I liked him.

After returning Mr. Rodriguez to his room, I lent my coworker, Martha, a hand in the laundry room. Martha was a middle aged, white woman from Montana. She was rugged and solitary. Most of the staff hated the repetitive nature of the laundry room, but Martha enjoyed it. She worked almost exclusively down there. No one really minded because we hated the job, and the laundry always got done, so why complain? I liked to sneak "extra" breaks by hanging out with Martha from time to time. Today was no different.

When I entered, Martha was folding a pile of sheets. A radio was playing oldies from around the corner. You couldn't hear the music clearly. You weren't supposed to. It was simply a more pleasant way of drowning out the laundry room noise. How Martha could enjoy it in there was beyond me. She was an obese woman; about five foot six, with wavy brown hair. I came up behind her and tapped her left shoulder. When she turned to see who it was, I hurried to the opposite side.

"Real mature," she mumbled. I smiled and hopped on the laundry table.

"What's going on, big Martha?" I asked.

"Just doing laundry, it's kind of my job. Maybe you should be doing yours." She always gave me crap for taking extra breaks.

"Martha, I've told you a thousand times, part of my job is making you happy. Now how can I do that if I don't come and check in on you from time to time?" I looked at her with a fake expression of concern.

"You could make me happy by not coming down here and bothering me," she said.

"I'd love to do that, but how would I know you were truly happy?" I asked.

"Guess you'd just have to take my word for it," she replied. I liked Martha. She had a dry sense of humor and hardly any feminine qualities to speak of. So in a way, it was like hanging with one of the guys. She had worked at Harrington's longer than me, and it showed. She didn't smile much anymore. The building had a way of melting your happiness. Maybe it was the ever-present fear of ending up a patient in a place like it? Who knows? We small talked for about ten minutes before she said something that caught my attention.

"I think I'm gonna quit," she said.

"Why?" I asked.

"Because I hate it, this job," she answered. "I hate waking up knowing that I'm going to spend eight or more hours, five days a week, in a basement doing laundry." She put the sheet down and looked at me. "I'm 42 years-old," she said, "I want more." She turned back to her pile of sheets. I sat quietly and watched her. She didn't say anything else.

Maybe it was the noises of the laundry room that made me wake up, or the dissatisfaction in Martha's voice, or hearing Mr. Rodriguez mourn his wife's breasts, but I realized the position I was in. I was surrounded by miserable people. Harrington's retirement center was full of employees who hated working there, and patients who hated living there. That meant everyone in Harrington's was either looking for a way out, a diversion from their daily lives, or help with accepting their confinement. No matter how you sliced it, I had a building full of miserable people, desperate for change. These people needed me. They needed my new Moosetian (or Moosewegian? Maybe he never settles on a name.) ways. I could show them the path to true happiness. Not to mention, I could use this opportunity to show Rachel what an effective leader I could be. "Who can't lead miserably desperate people?" I asked myself. When they see how happy Moose is, how carefree his life is, and how they can be just as happy and carefree by emulating him, they would be putty in my hands. "Let's see Sean lead a group of people to inner happiness," I thought to myself. Heck, this may even show Rachel the error she made in leaving me. Moose was the answer to everything.

If someone as sane and intelligent as myself could, on their own accord, decide to follow Moose's lead in life, then convincing an unstable person would be child's play. After Rachel saw how my patients and coworkers worshiped me for changing their lives, she'd leave Sean and run back to me, at which time I'd dump her in an effort to scar her for life. Some might have called my plan unMoosetian-like, or even sinister, but it seemed fair to me. I'd portray Moose as the prime example of personal fulfillment and harmony, and I'd teach others how to find the same balance in their lives. They'd be following my dog's values and priorities. He'd practically be a god to them, and if he was God, then I was

God's owner, which I'm pretty sure made me vice deity or co-God of this newly formed religion. I was essentially the Pope. I could make Harrington's the first congregation of Moose, and me its spokesman. Maybe it would be a success? Maybe it would be a disaster? Who could say for sure? Either way, it didn't matter. If I wanted to get Rachel back, and improve the lives of those I work with, I had to make them worship my dog.

FRIDAY 7:37 P.M.

I was so excited after devising my plan that, aside from evening pill distribution, the last few hours of my shift flew by. The highlight was no doubt giving Mrs. Hawkins her sponge bath. I know it sounds awful, but if she were twenty years younger, or if I were fifty years older...there'd be some generation gaps getting filled! A series of strokes may have left her partially paralyzed and suffered speech loss, but her eyes said something entirely different. I like to think she looked forward to bath time.

The lowlight of my shift was repeatedly escorting Mr. Rodriguez from Mrs. Rodriguez's room (again, no relation). He claimed he was only trying to give her some tapioca pudding, but I knew better. It starts with tapioca pudding, continues with butterscotch pudding, and then it turns into operation granny panties. It was annoying removing him from her room, but it was funny at the same time. I mean, everyone agrees that old people sex is disgusting and wrong, that's just a scientific fact, but I respected his diligence.

The worst part of the day, and every day for that matter, is the evening pill distribution. The senior citizens from floors one and two gather in the cafeteria for dinner. After they eat, they have to stay on the second floor while we, the staff, clean up. The cleanup usually takes thirty to forty-five minutes. During this time, the old people usually gather in the lounge and watch something like "Murder She Wrote." This gives them time to talk, relax, digest etc. The thing that sucks about this time is how placid and docile the elderly become. It's like having a room full of dead people with a television on full blast. It's creepy.

I drove home and thought more about my plan to win Rachel's affection back. Maybe I needed to think it through a little more. I mean, just because Martha was unhappy, and Mr. Rodriguez was slowly losing his mind, doesn't mean I could convince them to worship my dog. And if that's the only way I can get Rachel back, brainwashing distraught and feebleminded people, then maybe she's not worth having. But if I could share Moose's happiness with those people, didn't I owe them as much? The answer to this question would have to wait because as I pulled in the driveway, I noticed Rachel's car parked at the curb.

I opened the door and saw her on the couch patting Moose's big, brindle head. "What are you doing here?" I asked. "Did you knock before coming in?" She smirked at me and stood up.

"I come to tawk bout you and Sean, " she said. I patted Moose on the head while walking him to the back door.

"Good boy," I said while letting him outside. I turned back to Rachel. "There's nothing to talk about," I said, "I'm not mad at Sean. Actually, I'm sorry the whole thing happened." I sat on the couch and looked for Moose in the backyard.

"I happy to hear that," she said. "Sean said he pwess chawges ginst you, but I tell him you sahwee. I say I tawk wit you and fix it."

"Well, consider it fixed," I said. She smiled in appreciation. "I'm changing, Rachel," I continued. "Yep," I paused dramatically, "I'm starting to think me dumping you was a good thing. It was hard to do, but it gave me a chance to focus back on my career." I gazed out the window hoping to make my comments look and sound even deeper. I felt a twinge of guilt for being so convincing. "I think things are really going to start happening for me now. I'm gonna be a leader, Rachel. It's too bad it took us breaking up to remind me what I want in life." I slowly turned my view from the window to her.

"What you tawking bout?" she asked. "I gone one day. You still wash old people."

"Actually, Rachel, I just got a promotion." I tried to sell the lie with raised eyebrows and head nods.

"Pomotion to what," she asked, "diaper changa?" I stood in amazement.

"Where are you learning this stuff?" I asked her. "The breakup speech, now the snappy diaper comment? What happened to the Rachel I knew?" She locked eyes with me and put one hand on her chest.

"I'm not girl who rode boat over anymore," she said. I 'Merican woman now." I reached out and placed a hand on her shoulder.

"Rachel," I said, while returning her eye contact, "I'm sorry about the boat ride. It's like I said, I couldn't afford a..."

"It's not bout boat wide," she interrupted. She pulled away from my hand and stepped toward the door. "I should go," she said, "Sean wait for me."

I walked her to the door. Why is it when you break up with a woman, they automatically become ten times more attractive? She was definitely worth having! As I walked Rachel out, I could smell her perfume. It was subtle, but sexy. I could tell it was expensive because it only lingered in the air briefly. Good perfume, like a good woman, hangs around for only so long. My father taught me that. She turned around to say a final goodbye. Since my promotion lie had bombed, I needed to make up another accomplishment.

"Hey, I wasn't lying about good things happening to me at work. Matter a fact, if you want to see something cool, take a trip to Bryant Park Sunday afternoon." She tilted her head and smiled slightly.

"Why? What at Bryan park Sunday?"

I had no answer. "Ahh....well, Rachel, you'll see me leading a large group of people. I'm kind of in charge of the whole thing," I boasted vaguely.

"What thing?" she asked.

"Whoooaa... I can't give it all away now. You'll just have to come to the park this Sunday." I smiled and folded my arms. "I think you'll be impressed." She looked at me with a hint of curiosity.

"Okay," she said. "I see you there." She leaned in and gave me a hug. "Oh, one more thing," she said. I bent down to listen. "You no dump me, I dump you!" She kissed my cheek and walked toward her car. I shook my head. Where was she learning this stuff?

FRIDAY 8:12 P.M.

I went back inside the house. Moose was waiting at the back door. He licked my hand as he entered. "What the hell was I going to show her Sunday?" I thought to myself. I needed to speed up my plan.

"Come here boy," I called to Moose. He came with his mouth dripping from the water bowl. "Are you ready to become a god, boy?" I asked, while dodging the strings of slobber dangling from his mouth. "We've got to put on one hell of a show, Moosey." I rubbed his ears, he liked that. I had to think of something, and I had to think fast. Tomorrow was Saturday. That meant I had one day to convince a large group of people to follow me to a city park where they would glean life lessons from my dog. "Moose rule #2," I thought to myself, "make decisions from your heart, not your pride and genitals."

With my plan of religious conversion/brainwashing thrown into hyper-speed, I decided it wise to only rely on foolproof tactics from there on out. I had to play it safe. There wasn't time to think of wacky or creative ways of persuading people into following Moose. I had to use the three things everyone at Harrington's wanted; food, entertainment and a chance to get outside. "Going to Bryant Park took care of the latter," I said to myself, "but what about the food and entertainment?" I affectionately slapped Moose on the hind. "Don't worry, buddy. We'll think of something." He looked up at me and cocked his head to one side. He was a handsome dog. If any dog ever deserved to be made a deity, it was him. I grabbed a can of whipped cream and headed to bed.

SATURDAY 5:10 A.M.

The alarm awoke me with its high-pitched blaring and beeping. I glanced out my shadeless windows. There was no sunlight visible. Winter was approaching. I did my nude, morning stretch in front of the bedroom window. Getting up for work so early was awful. That's part of the reason I had the work schedule I had. I volunteered for the shift after Casey quit. Casey was the previous weekend guy at Harrington's. He quit a little over a year ago. No one wanted his shift, working forty hours in three days didn't sound too appealing to most of the staff. I took it so I'd only have to get up early three days a week. I only had to work three days a week for that matter also. The other four days were mine to do whatever the hell I wanted. But... to be completely honest...I didn't do anything special on those four days off. Besides the occasional barfly I'd take home, I did nothing most days off but go to the gym, walk Moose, and look at porn on my home computer- the American male's dream.

I let Moose out to do his morning duty and hopped in the shower. Somewhere between brushing my teeth and shampooing my hair, I had a brilliant idea. I could get the seniors at Harrington's to follow me by getting them to agree when they were least able to resist my request. And when would that be? It was such an obvious answer; I was both surprised and disappointed I hadn't thought of it earlier- evening pill distribution! They sit around in a food and pharmaceutical induced coma every evening after dinner. What I needed was to get them focusing on me all at once, and I think I knew how. I dried myself off and let Moose back inside. He walked past me and headed for his bowl.

"Today is the first day of your new life, Moose. That's right, buddy. After today, you'll no longer be just my dog- you'll be a spiritual leader." I peeked in the kitchen to see Moose's reaction. He wasn't there. He had circled back out into the living room and climbed onto the couch. I finished getting dressed and poured a bowl of cereal. Cap'n Crunch was still my favorite. Give me a bowl of Cap'n with crunch berries and I was good for a balanced breakfast. I turned on Sportscenter and watched last night's highlights. I'm not sure why, but watching sports gave me a chance to slow down and think. Half the time, I wasn't really watching the show; I was just giving my eyes something to focus on while I thought about other things. Today was no different. I had to be on top of my game if I was going to pull this thing off. I finished my bowl of cereal and watched a few more basketball highlights. "The concept of a team game is gone from today's basketball," I thought to myself. I was suddenly happy I didn't watch much basketball anymore. It was time to go. I looked at Moose on my way to the Kitchen.

"I'll be back around 7:30," I called to him while rinsing my bowl. "You're in charge till I return, okay, Big Guy? Guard the house with your life!" He only raised his eyebrows and slowly wagged his tail at my command.

Another good thing about my work schedule was that there's no traffic at 6:30 a.m. on a Saturday morning. When I worked the day shift last year, it sometimes took an hour to drive the fifteen miles to Harrington's. It was hard to believe how fast the city was growing. It was even harder to believe the city had done nothing to ease congestion on the roads. I had thought about riding a bike to work, but decided I'd rather bitch about the traffic than die from a smog related case of lung cancer. I was going to stop at a Walmart on the way to work. If I hoped to get the patients at Harrington's to focus on me, I was going to need something to grab their attention, something that appealed to all old people, something big...and I was sure Walmart had it. What was it? Matlock, on DVD. When everyone finished eating, I'd throw on an episode. They'd be intently watching old Ben Matlock piece together the case, and I'd interrupt by pausing the DVD and asking them to go with me to Bryant Park on Sunday. They'd be so stuffed from dinner, medicated, or interested in finishing Matlock, that they'd agree without even questioning why they were going. That was the beauty of old people; they were as predictable as children, or dogs. It's that same predictability that makes dealing with all three both illuminating and infuriating.

Walmart was only a few miles from my house. Come to think of it, Walmart was only a few miles from everyone's house. You couldn't drive more than two miles in one direction and not see a Walmart. For some reason the company just bothered me. I never liked places that sold both guns and milk. Something just made me uneasy about those two items being sold in such close proximity to one another. It seemed unnatural. Nonetheless, there I was walking through the parking lot. I knew I'd find "Matlock" inside. What can't you find inside Walmart? I wandered to the stereo, computer, music, video game, phone, camera, movies, MP3, C.D., LCD, DVD section. "Matlock" was in the bin labeled "television classics." It made me think when I saw some of the shows I grew up watching in the "classics" section. It made me feel older. It reminded me that nothing stops time. Every day I was a day closer to living at Harrington's myself. Time truly waits for no man. I also noticed there were no "Air Wolf" DVDs in the "classics section;" a great oversight by the Walmart brass is my opinion. I purchased the Matlock DVD, a breakfast burrito, and a pack of tube socks, before heading to work. I wish I could say the tube socks were a part of my big plan, but the truth was they weren't. They were just a really good deal. Twelve tube socks complete with green stripes for $3.99...too hard to pass up.

SATURDAY 6:51 A.M.

After I put the breakfast burrito in the staff microwave, I headed for my locker. I put the DVD and the tube socks in my locker. I knew why I had brought the DVD inside, but I couldn't say the same for the tube socks. Maybe I didn't want them to be stolen from my car? I heard the microwave "ding" in the distance. I closed my locker and latched the lock. When I turned, I saw Andy.

"Little late, ain't 'cha?" he asked.

"Actually, Andy, I'm a few minutes early. Why, is there a problem or something...cause I got a burrito in th..."

"You were supposed to relieve me an hour early today, remember?" he interrupted. "What happened to that, huh?"

He was right, I had promised to let him off early. Letting most people down wouldn't bother me, but Andy was a good guy. I was embarrassed by breaking my word to him. I had to make it up to him. "Andy," I said, "I'm sorry. I've been busy as hell lately. Tell you what; I'll give you a fresh pack of tube socks to make up for it."

By the time we finished our litigation, my burrito was cold. That was the bad news. However, the good news was Andy and I settled our dispute, and all it cost me was eight dollars and a bag of tube socks. I thought we both made out well.

I started my shift by doing a quick lap around the second floor. I had worked at Harrington's long enough to finagle my shifts exclusively to the second floor. Everyone wanted to work on the first floor, the showroom. It was an easy life on that floor. Residents were active and healthy. They were almost your friends. It made your job easy. Your main responsibility was simply hanging out with the seniors. There was less clean up, planning, and crowd control on the first floor. They could take care of themselves for the most part. I'd have to wait until someone died or quit to make the first floor. It was coming though.

I was officially on the clock by seven in the morning. While that was the morning shift at most jobs, it was basically the lunch shift in a retirement center. The majority of Harrington's residents started their day anywhere between 4 and 6 a.m. That means by the time I got there, most had already eaten and were starting their leisure activities. On my stroll around the halls, nothing significant struck my eye. Mr. Rodriguez was watching TV in his room, Mrs. Rodriguez was in hers, and the staff was finishing cleaning up breakfast. The most intriguing thing I could find was Mr. Corbit playing his guitar. Mr. Corbit was a seventy-something, thin, white man. He was about six feet tall, and only had hair on the sides of his head. His son had placed him in Harrington's ten months ago claiming he wasn't home enough to watch after his father. Two months after his submission to Harrington's, our staff doctor noticed Mr. Corbit had early colon cancer. Three months later, he had the cancerous portion of his colon removed. Ever since the surgery, Mr. Corbit has sat in his room and taught himself to play the guitar. He said beating cancer made him value the time he had left in life, so he set out to do some of the things he had always wanted to do. First on that list was learning to play guitar. I listened at his door before knocking. He was slowly plucking on a single string. I cringed at what sounded like a guitar being suffocated.

"How's it going today, Mr. Corbit?" I asked while tapping on his door. He was facing the window on the far side of his room. He turned around when he heard my voice. "Sounds like you're working on a new song there," I said jokingly. He rested the guitar on his lap and smiled at me.

"It's an old Jim Croce song," he said. "You probably don't know who Jim Croce was," he said while patting his thigh, "he was before your time."

"Shoot, Mr. Corbit, I know all about Jim Croce. He sang "Bad, bad Leroy Brown", "If I could save time in a bottle", and a bunch of other great songs. How young do you think I am?"

"You got me," he said. "I didn't think kids your age still knew good music. It's all loud and sexual now. No one sings anymore. Just a bunch of yelling." He had turned his attention back to the window.

"I hear you Mr. Corbit," I said. "Well I've got a few more people to check in on, okay? You keep practicing. Start learning your chords," I told him, "E, G, C, and D. You learn those and you're good. No more one or two string songs."

"I tried to learn G once," he told me, "but I forgot where to put my fingers. My hands can't move well enough for that stuff." I told him he was wrong and showed him a few finger stretches to help with his hands. I admired Mr. Corbit. Most people don't want to learn new things because they're scared they'll fail at them, but here was Mr. Corbit, seventy-something years old, trying to learn something new. That took courage. It made me think of things I had been putting off. I decided right then and there that after I finished this religious conversion, Rachel-winning, then Rachel-dumping thing, I was going to go hang gliding. I envisioned it being extremely peaceful.

After I left Mr. Corbit, I headed to the laundry room to see Martha. Since she was the person that had given me the idea in the first place, I thought it appropriate to start the Moose conversions with her. Sure enough, she was standing at her table folding sheets. I could suddenly see why she hated her existence and I felt slightly bad for her; however, this was not the time for empathy. I walked to her table and started helping her with the laundry.

"Morning," she said. "What brings you down here?" I picked up on our conversation from the day before.

"I was thinking about what you said yesterday, Martha. About hating your job and wanting more from life. I understand what you mean. And to be honest, Martha, I used to feel the same way. I just wanted to tell you how I got over those feelings." She looked at me suspiciously.

"You came all the way down here to tell me that? At 7:15 in the morning?"

"I couldn't wait," I told her. "You were the first thing on my mind. I came here as quick as I could." She was still staring at me suspiciously.

"Humph. And what's this wisdom you've come to give me?" she asked.

I stopped folding laundry and looked her in the eyes. "I know this is going to sound strange," I said, "but just hear me out." I went on to mostly lie about how Moose had helped me through a difficult time in my marriage, and how I was a better person because of it. I said he was the one creature that showed me how I needed to behave on a daily basis in life. I told her that ever since I began following Moose, I was happier with myself, like I had found my purpose. I quit speaking and waited for her response. She sat quietly with her arms folded.

"So you think I should get a dog?" she asked.

"No, no. I think you should meet my dog, Moose." She looked at me like I had said something crazy.

"Why should I meet your dog?" she asked.

"Because he'll make you feel better," I said. "Maybe I didn't describe how Moose helped me very well..." I went on to re-explain how Moose was special and why she should meet him, only this time I used more metaphors and tossed around flowery words like "energy" and "spirit". Her expression showed she was less impressionable than I had originally perceived.

"Nope, I don't think I need to meet your dog, but thanks for thinking of me," she said. I had to think fast. I couldn't lose Martha. The whole plan of impressing Rachel relied on being a leader, and I had already lost my first follower. If she didn't want to follow me, perhaps she could help me lead. She didn't have to know the entire plan, and I'm sure I could use some help.

"Martha, wait a second. Maybe you're right, maybe you don't need to meet Moose, but what about the rest of Harrington's? What if he could help others the way he helped me? Wouldn't you want to be a part of something like that?"

She sat down and rested her head in her hand. "What, exactly, are you asking me to do?" she said with squinted eyes.

SATURDAY 8:09 A.M.

It took a little longer than I expected, but I had convinced Martha to help me get the residents to Bryant Park on Sunday. I told her about studies that suggested older people often benefited from being around pets. Animals helped relieve stress, promote happiness, and help seniors get exercise. She agreed to help organize a short trip to the park for an afternoon of lunch and light walking. She even suggested we bring some bread to feed the ducks. I had her completely fooled as to my true intentions. At first, I was a little worried about Martha's refusal to convert to Moosetianity, but I later figured it may be more pleasing, visually, with Martha as a helper. If all went well, Rachel would see Martha as a high-class servant, like a chambermaid. I could live with that.

I still had ten hours to work before dinner. It was after dinner, at evening pill distribution, that I'd put on an episode of Matlock and bring my plan one step closer to fruition. So what was I going to do until then? I hated working my entire shift. Some people actually like to be busy at their jobs; they claim it makes the time go by faster. I never agreed with that. I believed being busy at work made your job even worse. I had always felt that way. I put more effort into avoiding work, than actually working. For example, at my first job as a bag boy at a local grocery store, I would always volunteer to round up the loose shopping carts in the parking lot. I'd push the carts from one side to the other until I found my way behind the store. Once there, I'd smoke a joint and throw rocks at empty bottles. That went on for seven months till some religious coworker saw me and told Mr. Warner behind my back. My first "real" job was

after I graduated from college. I was a social worker at an alternative school for emotionally disturbed youth, ages 7-15. The job paid well, but I hated it. I tried to be professional at first, but I started using my sick days more and more. I called in sick so often they forced me to verify my illness with a doctor's note. Needless to say, I couldn't get one, so they fired me. It wasn't a big deal though; most those kids were real assholes. Some of them just needed someone to talk to, someone they could trust. I wanted to be that person for them, but those other kids ruined it for me. I mean how long can you use being molested or losing your parents to drug overdoses as an excuse to be rude to the people trying to help you? They were so self-centered. The bottom line was I just wasn't appreciated enough at that job. I couldn't get fired soon enough. Harrington's was no different. I tried to make myself visible around mealtimes, pill distribution, and holiday festivities. The rest of the time, my goal was to be invisible.

After watching an hour and a half of daytime television with a sleeping resident, I took a trip to Mrs. Hawkins' room. She was lying in her bed watching an old western. I walked in and pulled a chair up next to her. "How you doing today, Mrs. Hawkins?" I asked. Her eyes said she was fine. "You looking forward to your sponge bath later today?" Again, her eyes spoke for her with a definite "yes." She tried to speak, but only emitted a soft moan. I wondered what was going on inside her head. She could talk, sort of, but she was embarrassed at how she sounded. I tried to imagine how frustrating every day of her life must have been. I small talked with her a little while longer before getting up to leave. I ended our conversation by inviting her to Bryant Park with us on Sunday. I doubted she'd be able to come along, but that's why I invited her. I didn't want her to feel left out.

SATURDAY 12:10 P.M.

Lunch seemed like it took forever to arrive. It was corned beef, salad, and tapioca pudding. It was also time for afternoon pill distribution. The afternoon meal and pill time was much more mellow than the evening meal and pill was. There were various reasons for this; some seniors didn't eat lunch, some didn't take noon pills, and some didn't leave their rooms again until dinner. This made lunch a vagabond type of crowd. I liked it. No stress. You'd be surprised how squirrelly old people can get waiting for their medication. That's what made the evening meal and pill time a mess. Irritable, prescription addicted seniors are not a very fun crowd to hang with.

I saw Mr. Rodriguez swallowing his pills in the back of the room. He had one hand on his walker; the other was holding a paper cup to his mouth. I walked over to him and lightly kicked his walker with my right foot. He finished swallowing his pills and looked at me. He smiled and gave me his usual facial expression of faint recognition. He knew he knew me, but he didn't know how he knew me.

"Christian?" he asked me in a hopeful tone.

"No, Mr. Rodriguez, my name's not Christian." I threw his paper cup away for him and walked by his side. He used a walker, but he could keep a good pace with that thing. We always had the same conversations. I liked that about Mr. Rodriguez, it was a safe feeling. After he asked my name, he'd ask if I was married, some days I said yes, other days I said no. The sincerity of my answer didn't matter. His asking was merely a leeway into his next question, "Have I ever told you about my late wife Erlina's breasts?" Again, my answer didn't matter, because he was going to describe her breasts whether I wanted to hear about them or not. Fortunately though, I didn't mind hearing about his dead wife's breast. For some reason the topic never got old to me. "They were like apples," he'd say, "the Lord had a hand in making something that perfect." Then he'd mumble some Spanish gibberish to himself.

Talking to Mr. Rodriguez brought to mind a timeless question, "Why are Hispanic men so horny?" It was like they lived to have sex. I mean I enjoyed sex as much as the next guy, maybe more, but Hispanic men put my libido to shame. Think about it, the stereotype is that Mexican men have tons of children, cheat on their wives, and constantly eye rape women. I can't say if all of those stereotypes are true, but I can say that I regularly see Hispanic men *in public* with unattractive, even fat women. While I never recommend taking uneducated, unattractive or fat women out in public, their doing so proves my point- Hispanic men are so naturally horny, they'll sleep with any woman. To be honest, I kind of admired their commitment. I had always equated sleeping with fat women to the classic, "If you were starving, would you eat ______ to survive?" scenario. It's a fair comparison. If you hadn't had sex for two years, would you sleep with a three-hundred-pound woman to bust out of that slump? Or, if you were dying of thirst, would you drink your own urine to survive? My answer to both questions, consequently, was, "I don't know... and I hope I never have to find out."

Changing the topic with Mr. Rodriguez was easy- he had dementia. There was no need to politely or slyly segue to another discussion topic. All you needed to do was ask a question, so that's what I did.

"Hey, can I ask you something, Mr. Rod-ri-guez?" He stopped talking and looked at me with a blank expression on his face. "How would you like to have lunch at Bryant park tomorrow afternoon?" I asked.

He blinked a few times, undulated his jaw, and said, "I think I'd like that. Yes." With that, he smiled and strolled away. I tried to imagine what he was thinking about as he plotted down the hall. Today appeared to be a good day for Mr. Rodriguez. He seemed happy. I was just glad it was so easy to get his agreement to eat at the park. I could use him as an example when bringing the idea up to the rest of the residents. I could say, "See, Mr. Rodriguez is coming, who else wants to come?" That would help, but it didn't guarantee more seniors would volunteer. Old people are extremely stubborn. Mr. Rodriguez was a popular resident, so it couldn't hurt to have him on my side.

I didn't do much the rest of my shift. I was putting together my speech for the residents. The more intriguing I made the events sound, the more they'd want to come. The more exciting I made Moose sound, the more likely they'd be willing to break their precious routines to go see him. That was going to be the hardest part of the scheme, getting them to break their routines. The worst quality of old people is their resistance to change... and their smell. I hope they cure both before I get old. In hopes of preparing the best dog-following pitch possible, I went to the staff bathroom for an extended bathroom break. I sat quietly on the oddly clean toilet and pondered the best way to present Moose and his alleged "uniqueness". I couldn't use the angle of self-reflection with a bunch of senior citizens; they're past the point of self-improvement. Half of them don't remember enough about themselves to change if presented with inspiration to do so. Most seniors barely remember who they are, tightly cling to their memories, or are merely trying to prolong the inevitable. Therefore, I needed an angle that combined a sense of familiarity and positive memories. However, it had to be presented as a limited time opportunity. They had to see it as something they *couldn't* miss. "What could tempt a group of ill and crotchety old people to venture all the way to a public park for lunch?" I asked myself. "And how could I work my dog into it all?" I didn't have to use the toilet, but something about sitting on it soothed me mentally. I ran through scenario after scenario before it finally struck me, and Moose was the answer again.

I left the restroom with these facts solidified in my brain: 1. Rachel didn't know in what capacity I was going to be leading the old people. All I told her was that I was being promoted at work, and as a result, I now had more of a leadership role. She was merely expecting to see me in charge of a group of people. She was coming to see me be a leader, like her beloved Sean. What I was actually leading was irrelevant. 2. Martha knew I was bringing Moose to Bryant Park. She also knew that I was going to tell people there was something special about my dog, and that they should meet him. While she didn't agree with my opinion of Moose, she had agreed to help me pull off the park field trip. And 3. Moose had to be the main attraction. As long as I operated under these three facts, I could keep everyone in the dark just long enough to pull this thing off. After we finish up at the park, I'd drop Moose back off at home, go back to Harrington's, give Mrs. Hawkins her sponge bath and head home to find Rachel waiting for me. She'd tell me how impressed she was at seeing me in control of all those old people and staff members. She'd then give me that look she used to give me when she first got off the boat before she asked to get a job to better her English skills. Then I'd have intense sex with her on the living room couch, after which I'd dump her. I felt confident as I returned to work. Toilet philosophy can do that for you.

SATURDAY 5:00 P.M.

By the time dinner finally rolled around, my heart was beating double time. I paced about the cafeteria as the residents ate. I was trying to detect their mood. Like any large group of people, you could often sense their emotions. This is a valuable skill in any crowded environment from public schools to prison. However, there was nothing to detect on this night. The residents calmly sat and ate their processed chicken pot pies. There were no spicy conversations taking place, no romantic gossip, nothing. I didn't know if the seniors' dull state was a good or bad thing. It didn't really matter either way. The time to act was quickly approaching. I went to get the Matlock DVD, and on the way back, I ran into Martha. She was on her way to the cafeteria from the laundry room. We stopped and talked in the hall. I wanted to tell her about Mr. Rodriguez already agreeing to go to the park with me. I guess I thought it would strengthen her commitment to helping me organize this whole park trip. However, this was before Martha informed me of her feelings for Mr. Rodriguez.

"He's a perv." she said. "All he does is stare at my breasts and try to seduce Mrs. Rodriguez with pudding." She looked at me as if waiting for some sign of agreement. I gave none. She continued, "He just gives me the creeps, and I'm not the only one. Good luck getting any of the female residents to go on this picnic with him going." I was shocked. I had never heard anyone talk about Mr. Rodriguez that way.

"Are you sure we're talking about the same Mr. Rafael Rodriguez?" I asked.

"Do we have another one?" she replied.

"Well, no," I said, "it's just that h..."

"Look," she interrupted, "I'm sure he's more likable for the male staff here, but you've got to understand, us women on staff, we see Mr. Rodriguez as a horny old man who, if he's not trying to cop a

feel or catch a peek, he's trying to jump his feeble wife's bones." She rested her hands on her meaty hips and looked at me a moment.

"Wait, are you talking about Mrs. Rodriguez?" I asked.

"Of course I am," she said, "who else does Mr. Rodriguez bring pudding two or three times a day?" I chuckled out loud to her question and answered with one of my own.

"You know they're not married, right?"

"They're not?" she asked.

"No. It's just a coincidence them sharing a last name. I thought they were married for a while too, but turns out his wife, who had perfect breasts by the way, according to Mr. Rodriguez that is, died over ten years ago."

"Really?" she said. "They're not married?"

"Nope. Crazy, huh?" We talked about that and Mr. Rodriguez in general, for a few minutes. I was sharing some of my favorite Mr. Rodriguez stories with her. Then we started discussing the plan. I was going to need her to drive one of Harrington's vans to the park. We were finalizing travel details when we noticed it was close to time for evening pill distribution. We headed toward the resident lounge.

SATURDAY 5:46 P.M.

By the time we got there, most of the seniors were done eating and receiving their pills. A few staff members asked where we had been. We answered a few of them with quick, safe alibis like folding laundry, or cleaning up a mess. Those were logical reasons to be tardy. We didn't answer a few coworkers questions because, well frankly, who the hell were they to ask? Nothing annoyed me more than people forgetting the chain of seniority. Don't question where I've been, or what I've been doing, unless you're my boss or in senior command, and none of these idiots were either. Martha wouldn't say it, but I'm sure she felt the same way.

Mr. Corbit was sitting next to Mr. Rash and Mrs. Flockspart. Mr. Rash was an old man from Pittsburgh. I'm sure someone would say he was a nice man, but I never got to know him. I never wanted to. Northeasterners generally come off as assholes. Mr. Rash was no exception. He had a loud voice and a nasty habit of touching people. Every conversation with him left you with ears ringing, and a feeling of molestation. Mrs. Flockspart was a retired kindergarten teacher. She was the complete opposite of Mr. Rash, and I never understood why she hung around him. She had a soft sweet voice. I enjoyed hearing her talk.

The lounge was filling up with residents expecting to watch television. I took a deep breath and grabbed the floor. I had one chance to win Rachel back, and this was the beginning of that chance. I slapped my hands together to get everyone's attention. The seniors who could hear me stopped talking and looked at me. The ones who couldn't hear me noticed the other seniors quieting down and did the same.

"If I could get everyone's attention," I began. "I have a little treat for you guys tonight." I reached into my uniform's oversized, turquoise front pocket. I pulled out the Matlock DVD and said, "Ta-dah." They seemed less than impressed. "It's a Matlock DVD," I announced. "I thought you guys might enjoy watching an episode or two. And after you finish, I've got a few surprises for you." Martha glanced at me with a hint of curiosity. I put the DVD in and sat on the rear counter. Martha came and stood next to me.

"What are these *surprises* you're going to share with them?" she asked me.

"Oh, nothing too big," I said. She looked at me with an expression that lacked tolerance or patience. "Calm down," I said, "it's nothing to worry about."

"What's the surprise?" she asked again. I could tell she didn't like where this was going.

"Martha, all I'm going to tell them is we're going to Bryant Park for lunch tomorrow. That's all... and that they can meet Matlock's dog there."

"What?" she said, turning and cutting me with her eyes. "Matlock's not even a real person," she continued. "Why don't you promise Mickey Mouse while you're at it?"

"First of all, Martha, Mickey Mouse is lame! I mean why does he wear shoes, shorts and gloves, but no shirt? Talk about creepy. And second of all, I know Matlock isn't real. I just need a way of involving Moose in all this." She stood silent a moment, as if deciding what to say.

"I thought you wanted the residents to see how great your dog was. How simple, yet happy his existence was. You were using him to inspire change in their lives. Where does Matlock's dog fit into that?" she asked.

I was most impressed with how closely Martha had paid attention to my words. She recalled not only the words I had said about Moose, but she even captured the emotion I had tried to express. She was brighter than I had given her credit for. Nonetheless, I needed to lie to her again.

"You're right, I want them to meet Moose to inspire change, however, I thought saying he was Matlock's dog might excite them some. I thought it might bring a few extra people out to the park. That's not such a bad thing, is it?" I posed my question with a gentle shoulder shrug and eyebrow raise.

"So you're going to lie to them?" she asked.

"Come on, half of them won't remember being lied to in the first place," I said. "I'm just bending the truth a little." It was obvious she didn't agree with me, but for whatever reason, she didn't voice anymore objections.

"This isn't a good idea." she said.

"Martha, relax. What harm can it cause?"

The episode of Matlock was about a doctor who killed a patient in an effort to cover up their affair. Ben Matlock was a smooth operator. He'd peruse around the crime scene and find details the police had overlooked. If Matlock happened to miss something, his private investigator, Tyler Hudson, would find it for him. Then they'd put the pieces together with the help of Matlock's daughter, Charlene Matlock, and send the bad guy to jail. I could understand why old people enjoyed watching Matlock work. He was an old, gray-haired man catching younger people in lies. He would outsmart people ten, twenty, even thirty-years his junior. That had to be appealing to old people. I never dug Matlock. I was more of a Jim Rockford fan myself. I liked his humor and renegade style. A private eye is more of a loose cannon when compared to an elderly, southern lawyer, and that interested me more. Maybe I'd become a Matlock fan as I aged? I shuddered at the thought.

With a glance around the room, I saw the faces fixated on the screen. It was time to act. Matlock had made it clear he knew the doctor was guilty, and he was tightening the screws on him. The seniors were absorbed in the drama. Personally, I never liked the way Matlock pestered his suspects. Columbo did the same thing, but at least he was humorous while doing so. It was about twenty minutes into the show when I paused the DVD.

"Could I get everyone's attention?" I began. Heads turned and looked at me in confusion. They were still trying to figure out what had happened to the show. "You all enjoying Matlock?" I asked. They mumbled yes in response. "Good," I said, "I'm glad you're enjoying it. Well guess what guys, I showed you Matlock for a reason today. Who wants to do something special tomorrow?" I asked. I saw two hands rise in my peripheral vision. It was the response I was expecting. They'd change their mind when they heard the details. "Well, for those of you who want to come, we'll be having lunch at Bryant Park tomorrow, where you can meet... Ben Matlock's dog!" I braced myself for the excitement sure to fill the room. I heard quiet murmurs throughout the room. Things like, "Matlock's dog..." "Ooh, lunch..." and "I like the park," circulated in the room. I took back control of the floor by saying, "Come talk to me or Martha after Matlock if you want to go tomorrow. We'll be organizing the activity. We've already got Mr. Rodriguez on board; we need some more people." I could see some of the residents weren't sold on the idea yet, so I added, "When will you get another chance to meet Matlock's dog? Again, find me or Martha after the show if you want to go." I hit play on the DVD and walked back by Martha.

"They could hardly contain themselves," she said.

"Don't worry, all we need's a few," I replied.

SATURDAY 6:28 P.M.

After two episodes of Matlock, the lounge started to empty out. I found myself in a bind. I wanted to hang in the lounge with Martha and recruit people for the picnic with Matlock's dog, but I only had two minutes before Mrs. Hawkins' sponge bath. I had ended my shift with Mrs. Hawkins sponge bath ever since I took over the weekend slot. It was a nice, calm way to end the day. I like to think it helped end her day too.

The only seniors left in the lounge after Matlock were Mr. and Mrs. Rodriguez (no relation), Mr. Corbit, and Mr. Rash. I was disappointed in the turnout. Harrington's management liked outings to have at least five seniors participate. I had to find one more person to come. However, that would have to be done later. I needed to get to Mrs. Hawkins' bathing session. I asked Martha if she could explain when they needed to be ready for the vans without my help. She reluctantly said she could but asked where I was off to in such a hurry.

"We've only got four people to go so far," I said. "We need one more person, and I know just who to ask." I winked at her in an attempt to look both secretive and cool, before turning and running down the hall. I think I pulled it off.

By the time I got to Mrs. Hawkins' sponge bath, she was already in the tub. There were two other staff members in there with me, Ruben and Amanda. Technically, they were the two who were assigned to give Mrs. Hawkins her bath. Harrington's liked there to be two staff members in those types of environments. That way one can verify or monitor their partner's actions. Ruben was the only male staff member regularly assigned to bathe female residents. I'm not sure why that was, but I assumed the answer was related to affirmative action. Even though I wasn't assigned to be at Mrs. Hawkins' sponge baths, I made them a ritual when I worked. Ruben complained the first few times I watched him bathe her, but I quickly pulled seniority on him. I told him I had been supervising Mrs. Hawkins' baths long before he joined Harrington's staff, and if he wanted to take it up with his superior, me, he could do it. That seemed to shut him up. Besides, I told him; even though my presence wasn't required it was Mrs. Hawkins' preference that I'm there. She felt safe with me watching. I was her bath time guardian. Whether that was true or not was irrelevant. I only said it because I knew that would shut Ruben up. He was always in favor of whatever the residents wanted. "This is their home," he'd always say. Or "Our job is to make them as comfortable as possible." I assured him Mrs. Hawkins was most comfortable when I watched her bathing from across the room. "This isn't about me," I had once told him, "this is about making Mrs. Hawkins happy." He never pressed the issue after that.

When I walked in Mrs. Hawkins' room, she was already in the tub, and her red hair was tucked in a shower cap. She rested in Ruben's hands, while Amanda sponged her arms. I entered from the rear and patted Ruben on the shoulder. Amanda looked up and smiled at me.

"Sorry I'm late guys, I got tied up with some stuff after dinner." I changed my gaze from Ruben and Amanda to Mrs. Hawkins. "How are you tonight Mrs. Hawkins? You know I got here as fast as I could, right?" Ruben and Amanda exchanged looks. "Nothing's gonna keep me from your sponge bath," I continued. Mrs. Hawkins blinked at Amanda. "So what are you guys talking about?" I asked. They both seemed to hesitate before Ruben spoke.

"Nothing much," he said. "What did you have to handle after dinner?" he asked. I smiled at his question because it provided me with a natural segue into asking Mrs. Hawkins if she'd like to come on the trip with me. I sat on the edge of the tub and settled myself before answering.

"Well, Ruben, that's part of the reason I hurried here so quickly."

"What was the other part of the reason?" blurted Amanda.

"What was that, Amanda?" I looked at her with a cold stare. I had heard what she said, and she knew as much, but this wasn't about that. I was giving her the kind of stare that said, "Are you big enough to say that again?" Amanda was a young white girl, with long auburn hair. She had a slim build. She was one of those "earthy" girls who wore pieces of wood in her hair and laughed at everything. "Did you say something, Amanda?" I asked again.

"No." she said. "I was just... I mean... nothing." she giggled and started sponging Mrs. Hawkins' legs. That's the problem with free spirits; they don't always follow the correct protocol. She hadn't worked at Harrington's for more than two months, and she's already attempting to give me crap about me getting my 83-year-old voyeurism on? Who did she think she was? It took Ruben around a year to start asking why I liked to watch or help bathe Mrs. Hawkins. I told him it was a tradition. In hindsight, that probably wasn't the best idea, but the point is, he did his time before challenging me or my actions. That's how a pro does it. Amanda needed to learn that lesson.

"Anyway, as I was saying," I continued with emphasis, "we were talking about taking a few of the residents on a special lunch trip tomorrow. That's right. We're going down to Bryant Park to eat lunch outside, and that's not the best part." I looked deep into Mrs. Hawkins' eyes, "We may get to meet a celebrity also." I stopped explaining any further details to feed the curiosity I had so beautifully developed.

"What celebrity?" Ruben asked as if on cue.

"Great question, Ruben. Are you ready for this Mrs. Hawkins? How would you like to meet Matlock's dog?" I waited for Mrs. Hawkins' response.

"Who's Matlock?" Amanda asked Ruben.

"It's a TV show," Ruben said. "The residents like to watch it after dinner sometimes."

"That's right they do," I said, "and I pulled some strings and got his dog to meet us at the park for lunch. You're more than welcome to come, Mrs. Hawkins." I smiled at her shyly.

"Wait, is Matlock a real person?" asked Amanda. I swatted her question aside as ridiculous and helped Ruben stand Mrs. Hawkins up. Amanda got a towel and dried her off. I waited for them to put her in a wheelchair and head back to her room before I invited her again.

"So I'll come grab you before we get in the van and head to the park, okay Mrs. Hawkins?" She looked at me and blinked twice. "You'll have a great time, I promise." I rested my hand on her shoulder and squeezed lightly.

"Isn't your shift over now?" Amanda asked with a giggle.

"Yes, Amanda, it is. I was just saying good-bye. Do you have a problem with that?" I gave her the same cold stare I had given her earlier.

"I was just wondering," she mumbled. I glared at her a few moments longer before saying goodnight to Ruben and Mrs. Hawkins. Amanda was quickly getting on my nerves.

SATURDAY 7:04 P.M.

I walked back to the staff locker room and changed clothes. There was a note in my locker from Martha that said she had gotten a van reserved for tomorrow. The note also said we'd meet in front of Harrington's at 11 a.m. I crumbled the note up and threw it away. I got dressed and smiled at how organized Martha was. It seemed like women were always more organized than men. I remembered being in middle or high school and always joining the girls' group for projects or assignments. It seemed like I was doing the same thing with Martha's help on this field trip. Interesting.

Moose was asleep on the couch when I came home. I sometimes took for granted the luxury of Moose being able to hold his bowels for over twelve hours. When he was a puppy, he would piss and shit all over the house. It didn't matter if I was gone for five minutes or five hours, he would put a new stain on the carpet. There was a time that I left him outside all day, but he got too hot. So I had to buy a huge cage to put him in when I was gone. Rachel used to watch him before she got her job at Sean's office. She said she wanted to learn English better and thought a part time job would help. I should have been more suspicious of her getting a secretary job. I mean come on; she can hardly speak English two years after taking the job. I doubt Sean hired her for her typing proficiently or phone skills! Anyway, after she started working, Moose would spend hours in the cage I bought. Then when I'd come home, I'd let him outside to use the restroom. He got used to the routine, and the cage was put in the garage after six or seven months. I only thought about his bowel control after coming home from twelve- or sixteen-hour shifts. I was kind of amazed Moose could hold it so long. I sure as hell couldn't hold in a piss for that long. I smiled as I let him in the backyard. He really was a great dog. Maybe he could make some of the seniors happy tomorrow. I watched Moose do his usual routine of sniffing, spinning, then pissing and shitting.

I left Moose in the backyard and went to the kitchen to grab a beer from the fridge. There was a message on the phone from some college loan debt collector. I couldn't believe they were still harassing me after all these years. I had no intention of paying back my college loans. I went to a public university. I never understood why a public education is free for kindergarten through 12th grade, but costs thousands of dollars after high school. I understand charging for private colleges, they paid for the isolation, but a public university is just the conclusion of the free American education system. Why should I have to pay for it? I know I signed various forms agreeing to repay the loans, but I think my argument trumps my signature.

I let Moose back inside and sat on the couch. We watched TV for a little over an hour before I started to feel tired. Sunday was a monster of a day without the field trip to the park. Sunday was my sixteen-hour shift. I got to work at 7 a.m. and left Harrington's at 11 p.m. It makes for a long, long day. The trip to the park and bringing Moose in, that'll make the day go by faster if anything. I took a shower and headed to bed. I stopped to discuss tomorrow's plan with Moose first. He was back on the couch. Dogs need so little to be happy. Another lesson I could learn from Moose.

Now when I told Moose the plan, I didn't think he was truly listening to me or anything crazy like that, it was more for me. It gave me a chance to go over the scene one more time before tomorrow. I decided I would go to work for a few hours, leave once Martha got everyone in the van, head home, grab Moose, and go to Bryant Park. After we unloaded everyone, the seniors would sit down to eat lunch. When they finished eating, I'd bring Moose around to meet them one by one. Rachel would sit somewhere in the distance and watch the way I led everything. Once the seniors got back in the van, she'd come out of the woodwork and tell me how impressed she was with the way I controlled everything. She'd be a little turned on and follow me home to drop Moose off. I'd give her some quick secret sex while Martha and the seniors waited in the van. Once we finished the quickie, Rachel would be completely hooked and intent on getting back with me. I'd then return to Harrington's, finish my shift, come home, let Moose out, let him back in, and then go to bed prepared to deal with Rachel's newfound lust on Monday morning. It was less complicated than it sounded, I was sure of that. Rehearsing the plan set my mind at ease, and I went to my bedroom feeling good about the next day.

SUNDAY 5:10 A.M.

The alarm sounded at its normal time, but I was already awake. I laid in bed a good twenty minutes before it went off. It was Sunday, D-day. I let Moose in the backyard to take care of his morning business. I left him out extra-long because I didn't want him dropping any Moose cakes in front of the Harrington residents; Mr. Rodriguez, Mr. Rash, Mrs. Rodriguez, Mr. Corbit, and the lovely Mrs. Hawkins. I had a feeling everything was going to go well. While Moose was outside, I watched the news and ate a bowl of cereal. The news didn't tell me anything special or helpful. The one good bit of information I received was that it was going to be a nice day. The forecast was sunny and clear. It seemed things were already going my way. Moose came in and sat beside me on the couch.

"Are you excited, boy?" I asked him. He wagged his tail, which I took to mean yes. "Well here's how it's going to go, buddy." I again ran through the same plan I told him last night. I wanted him, and myself more accurately, to be ready for the events of the day. Moose appeared ready and nonchalant about the whole thing. I liked his attitude. Again, I made a mental note to copy his behavior.

I spent the rest of my morning making my lunch and getting dressed. If we were going to the park for lunch, that meant I couldn't eat the food at Harrington's for lunch. I'd actually have to make my lunch. I made a turkey sandwich, packed an apple, a handful of chips, and a cream soda. It wasn't a big lunch, but I doubted I'd have time to eat anything anyway. I gave Moose a long head rub before heading out the door. I was excited to introduce the seniors to Matlock's dog... or Moose... whichever you preferred. Meeting him may be the last highlight of their lives. They could share the story with their family. It wasn't all bad, what I was doing. I was helping them get out into the sun for a couple of hours, and I was giving them the chance to meet a celebrity... sort of. I wouldn't lose any sleep over the affair, and that's what mattered. Well, that and ultimately crushing Rachel for following her heart.

The drive to work was typical- no traffic and still dark. I parked in my usual spot and entered Harrington's through the back door. Andy didn't work Sundays, so I wouldn't be running into him today in the locker room. He requested Sundays off so he could attend church with his family. I figured it was his southern tradition that made church so important to him. Not that church or religion wasn't important in our part of the country, but nothing compares to a Southerner's devotion. The South was called the Bible Belt for a reason. It was the only part of the country that willingly lived a hundred years in the past. Where else in America are you permitted to segregate Monday through Saturday, prohibited from buying alcohol on Sundays, and encouraged to pretend nothing unusual is taking place? The South is a strange land, and Andy was one of its children. He was likable though. He didn't press Jesus on others too much. That was what we "normal" Americans hated most about southerners, their persistent attempts to convert or include the Lord into other people's lives. It just comes off as antiquated and self-serving.

SUNDAY 7:00 A.M.

I started my shift by walking to Mr. Corbit's room. I wanted to touch base with all five of the seniors who would be going to the park with me, and Mr. Corbit was the closest. I knocked on his door lightly and entered. He was facing the window playing his guitar. "How are you doing, Mr. Corbit?" I asked. He turned to look at me and smiled. "Are you excited about meeting Matlock's dog later today?" I asked.

"I am looking forward to today," he said. "It'll be nice to eat outside, and I can't wait to talk to Matlock's *dog*." He had a strange emphasis on the word "dog" that I didn't understand.

"Hey, tell me if you know this song," he said before strumming a few notes I faintly recognized.

"You got me, Mr. Corbit. I give up, what song is it?"

"That was "No Woman No Cry," by Bob Marley," he said proudly. "I've been trying to learn some songs the youth listen to."

"That song is around 40 years old, Mr. Corbit. It's not exactly the youths' song anymore." He said he knew the song was old, but he had seen on the news that young people listened to Bob Marley while smoking "wacky-tabacky." He then went on to tell me that besides playing guitar, he had added "getting in touch with the youth" to his list of things to do before he died. He said some more stuff, but I started thinking about the kids at the skatepark. I wondered if they listened to Bob Marley. I'd have to ask them the next time I mooched some weed off them. I knew I could buy my own sack, but that would make me a certified drug user. I felt much more comfortable occasionally trading shitty malt liquor for a joint or pipe hit. That way I got something from them, and they got something from me. Barter and trade, it's the American way. Before I left his room, I reminded Mr. Corbit when to meet downstairs to load up in the van. He said he wouldn't forget and went back to playing his guitar.

I stepped into the hall headed for Mrs. Rodriguez's room. She was a quiet woman who spoke broken English. I could see why Mr. Rodriguez was crazy about her. I'm sure she was quite pretty in her younger years. She wore red most days, and this day was no different. She was watching some show on the Mexican channel. I knocked on her door and said hello. I spoke to her with terrible Spanish, and she responded to me in awful English. Through it all, we somehow managed to confirm her presence at the park that afternoon. I said, "Hasta luego" and left her room. I'm sure she was a nice lady, but I had never gotten to know her. Never really wanted to either. I think it was because it was so hard to talk with her. Her English was poor, and my Spanish was pathetic, so it made communicating difficult. Everything I knew about her, I learned from Mr. Rodriguez. She sounded lovely from his description. He said, "She was the wind that lifts his hair in the morning." I thought of asking him to explain his metaphor, but he spoke English so well, I figured he deserved poetic license.

With those two confirmed, I only had Mr. Rodriguez, Mr. Rash, and Mrs. Hawkins to go see. Of these three, only Mr. Rash was still up in the air. Mr. Rodriguez was a done deal. He was the first to agree to come, and Mrs. Rodriguez was going, so he was in for sure! Mrs. Hawkins was a lock as well. I had invited her myself, and everyone knew we had a special bond, so she was definitely going. With that in mind, I skipped Mr. Rodriguez's and headed for Mr. Rash's room.

Mr. Rash's room was on the far end of the building. He had a corner room. I didn't talk to him much because I always felt he was rude. He'd talk real loud to you with that awful Pittsburgh accent of his. Normally I'd go my entire shift without speaking to him, but I wanted to ask him a question. I was curious why he said he'd go in the first place. He didn't usually take part in field trips, or dances, or anything fun. He was a grouch. I knocked on his door, but no one answered. I looked inside his room and saw it was empty. I asked a couple staff members, and they told me he was still eating breakfast in the cafeteria. Mr. Rash was sitting at a small table by himself. He was eating eggs benedict. I sat down across from him.

"How are you doing this morning, Mr. Rash?" I asked. He smiled at me and finished chewing his mouthful. He wiped his lips before he spoke.

"What do you want?" he asked in a harsh, gravel voice.

"Good morning to you too," I mockingly said to him. "The reason I'm sitting with you, Mr. Rash, is to make sure you're still going to the park with us. So, are you still going to the park to have lunch and meet Matlock's dog?" He finished chewing another mouthful and swallowed slowly. Then he shoved another in his mouth.

"I wouldn't miss it for the world," he said with flecks of eggs shooting from his mouth. I looked at him with interest and thought it fair to ask.

"I'm just curious Mr. Rash, but why are you going on this trip?" He smiled at me again and looked up from his plate.

"Because I love watching train wrecks." He smirked and resumed eating. I stood up from the table and headed for the laundry room. "You know Donald Corbit keeps making a racket with that damn guitar of his," Mr. Rash hollered after me. "Won't stop playing it!" For whatever reason, Mr. Rash had a great disdain for Mr. Corbit. I never knew why. But he complained about him whenever he had the chance. "You should have never taught him to play that damn thing!"

Feeling the need to defend Mr. Corbit, and my guitar tutelage, I came back at him. "Actually, Mr. Rash, I think it's pretty cool he wants to learn new things. It's better than sitting around becoming a cranky old man." I smiled at him sarcastically and headed again for the laundry room. "Because I love train wrecks," I mimicked in the best old man voice I could, while walking down the hall. I couldn't stand that guy. We had never had a positive interaction the entire time I had worked at Harrington's. He was impossible. Simply put, Mr. Rash was nothing but an old bully with Lupus. I wasn't going to let him ruin my day.

I put a smile on my face and headed to Mr. Rodriguez's room. He was staring blankly at the floor when I entered. He had on gray sweatpants and a plain white tee shirt. He looked sad, but you could never tell with dementia patients; one minute they're angry, the next they're happy. It was a guessing game at best. I entered softly.

"Are you okay Mr. Rodriguez?" I asked. He looked at me and paused before answering.

"Don't tell me...Michael, right?" I pulled a chair up next to him.

"No, Mr. Rodriguez, my name's not Michael." He smiled and started looking at the floor again. "Are you ready to go to the park today?" I asked him in a happy voice. He looked back at me with a confused expression on his face.

"What park?" he asked. I had a feeling this would happen. Mr. Rodriguez's mental state was all over the chart during any given week. I knew it was possible he would forget that he agreed to have lunch at the park with us, that's why I had a plan. I'd mention Matlock's dog and Mrs. Rodriguez being at the park. That would do the trick. I scooted my chair closer to him.

"Remember, you said you'd have lunch at the park today with me and Martha, and Mrs. Rodriguez." His head shot up. Judging from his reaction, there was no need for me to even mention Matlock's dog being there, Mrs. Rodriguez was enough.

"I don't remember," he said softly, "but if Laquita is going, I'll go too.

"Who's Laquita?" I asked.

"Mrs. Rodriguez," he answered quickly. I was both amazed and a little jealous.

"What's my name, Mr. Rodriguez?" I asked.

He looked at me a long minute then said, "Michael?" I reminded him that I had just told him my name wasn't Michael. He said he couldn't remember my name and went back to staring at the floor. I held it together long enough to thank him for having lunch at the park with us. However, I left his room in a foul mood. How could he remember Mrs. Rodriguez's first name? I didn't even know her first name! And how could he always forget my name? I had taken care of him the last three years of his life. That's twice as long as he had known Mrs. Rodriguez. It didn't make sense. It just goes to show how complex the human brain is. That's what I told myself anyway.

SUNDAY 8:11 A.M.

Having talked to all the day's participants, except Mrs. Hawkins, I went to find Martha in the laundry room. I didn't feel it necessary to talk with Mrs. Hawkins before telling Martha everything was ready to go. Again, Mrs. Hawkins would be delighted to go to the park if for no other reason than the fact that we could spend some extra time together. Quality time. She loved being in my company, and I enjoyed being in hers. We got each other. I walked in the laundry room expecting to see Martha's husky frame, but she wasn't there. I asked around and finally found out that Martha had called in sick. I was instantly angry beyond description. I bet she called in sick on purpose. She hadn't liked my plan from the beginning. Now she was standing me up on the day of most importance. Well I wasn't going to let her mess the trip up. I was still going to take those seniors to the park, and they were still going to think Moose was Matlock's dog, and Rachel was still going to see the way I handled everything and everyone and want me back! I had put too much planning into this to just quit because Martha called in sick. I left the laundry room in a rush.

I collected my thoughts in the staff bathroom. I still had management's permission to take the seniors to the park, and I still had a van reserved to do so. The obstacles in my way were the fact that Harrington's management liked there to be at least two staff members on outings with five or more residents, especially different sexed staff members for bathroom issues and whatnot. I thought about rescheduling the event for next weekend, but even thinking about it made me feel like a failure. It had to be today. Rachel was waiting for word from me as to when to go to Bryant Park. If I told her it had been canceled, she would laugh at me. She'd see me as the same loser she saw me as before. I couldn't afford for that to happen. I'd have to pull this thing off alone. So I sat on the staff toilet and put together a plan that would allow me to get the company van, and the seniors in it by 11:30 am. It wasn't going to be easy, but if anyone could do it, it was me. I pulled my pants up, flushed, and left the bathroom feeling like a man on a mission. Toilet philosophy can do that to you.

I walked from the bathroom and went to the room where we kept the van keys. You might think a room such as this would be closely guarded, but you would be wrong. Harrington's was the type of place that only made security changes when events forced it to. Since there had never been any breaches of security, the van keys were in a cabinet in the staff offices on each floor. No one was in there, so grabbing a key was much easier than I thought it would be. I signed a sheet stating that I had taken the keys, and what time I would be leaving. With that part of the plan over with, I breathed a little easier. All that was left now was killing three more hours before pulling the van around front and loading the seniors in it. Mrs. Hawkins would be the most difficult because she would need a wheelchair.

Thinking of Mrs. Hawkins reminded me that I hadn't stopped by her room yet. I knew she wanted to go on the trip, but I should still make sure. I walked slowly to her room. When I got there, Amanda was by her bed.

"What are you doing here?" I asked. "Your shift doesn't start for another seven hours." She held Mrs. Hawkins' hand and looked me in the eyes. For once she wasn't giggling.

"I heard about the little field trip you want to take Mrs. Hawkins on," she said, "and I came in early to stop you." She smiled at Mrs. Hawkins and looked back at me.

"What are you talking about, Amanda? She's getting a chance to meet Matlock's dog, why would you want to take that away from her? Maybe you're too young to know this, but old people love Matlock... and his dog." She cocked her head to one side and shook it slowly.

"I'm not letting Mrs. Hawkins go," she said.

"What are you, her mother?" I quipped. "She's going to meet Matlock's dog, and you're just gonna have to deal with it." I smirked at her and walked toward Mrs. Hawkins' bed. "How are you doing Mrs. Hawkins?" I asked. "Don't worry, I'm not going to let Amanda ruin this day for you." It was sometimes hard to tell what Mrs. Hawkins was feeling or thinking. Her paralysis had made her eyes the main indicator of her emotions and thoughts. She was looking at me with wide eyes. I took that to mean she was taken back by all the commotion Amanda had caused. I tried to make her feel more at ease by asking Amanda to leave the room.

"I'm not going anywhere!" she replied with an unusual amount of attitude.

"Amanda, you're clearly upsetting Mrs. Hawkins and she's got a big day ahead, so why don't you take a hike." I glared at her with the same expression I had given her the day before. Her Auburn hair was pulled back behind her shoulders. I wasn't used to seeing her serious for this long. I would have been impressed by her nerve on most days, but this was not the time for her to "grow a pair." I had too much at stake. "So, what's it gonna be, Amanda? You gonna continue to upset Mrs. Hawkins with your arguing, or are you gonna help de-stress the situation by leaving the room?" I gently grabbed her arm and led her to the door. "After all," I continued, "isn't what's best for Mrs. Hawkins most important?"

She snatched her arm away from me and looked at Mrs. Hawkins with obvious concern. "This isn't over," she said before leaving the room. I watched her walk down the hall and around the corner. What was her deal? Why did she want to keep Mrs. Hawkins from going on this trip? I couldn't find the answers to those questions, so I stopped thinking about them. I had better things to think about; like how to get Mrs. Hawkins, wheelchair and all, along with four other senior citizens, into a van without Martha's help. It wasn't going to be an easy task.

The next two hours of my shift were the longest two hours of my entire life. I passed the time by walking around the halls pretending to look busy. I carried stacks of paper from one room to another, acting as if they had important information on them. I walked with mops like I was hurrying to clean up messes. I pushed wheelchairs up and down the hall. I did everything you could do at Harrington's, but actually work. Tons of people do the same every day at their jobs. That's the funny thing about work, most people hate it. No matter how many luxury cars you own, or bedrooms you have in your house, you can't escape the fact the humans were intended to lounge in savanna grasslands. The work environment triggers this recessed biological trait. Truth be told, I spent most of my workday figuring out ways to avoid having any duties or responsibilities. I just wanted the paycheck. But this day was different. I wanted to avoid work temporarily, so I could take on real responsibility later. I was taking five seniors' lives in my hands. And if that wasn't enough responsibility, I was also going to pull off a poorly planned farce in order to win my wife's materialistic heart back. When you looked at it that way, two hours of avoiding what was expected of me kind of made sense. I deserved as much.

SUNDAY 10:23 A.M.

With the van key in my possession already, I decided it time to gather the group. I started with Mr. Corbit. I went into his room, interrupting his rendition of The Fine Young Cannibals', "She Drives Me Crazy." "Trying to get in touch with the youth again?" I asked before telling him to wait in the lounge for me. He said he would put on his jacket and head to the lounge. He was still playing when I left his room.

Next, I went to Mrs. Rodriguez's room. She was sitting in the same place and watching what appeared to be the same show as when I had seen her last. I never understood Mexican shows or music. I mean obviously I didn't speak Spanish, but that wasn't what I meant. I mean everything looks and sounds the same. All the television shows have bad acting with weird characters that have way too many close ups, and all the music sounds like something you'd hear at a circus. Don't get me wrong, it's a wonderful culture, just not very creative. Even their food is all the same, tortilla, rice, beans, meat. You can change the way those things are served, but it's still those four ingredients with salad on top. Mrs. Rodriguez smiled at me when I knocked on her door. With a few hand signals and a whole lot of Spanglish, I told her to wait for me in the lounge. She smiled at me again and nodded. I held her door open as she grabbed a light shawl and left the room. She had a feminine quality about her walk. It was soft and submissive. I could see why Mr. Rodriguez dug her the way he did.

Speaking of Mr. Rodriguez, it was his room I was headed to next. He was napping in a chair. I lightly kicked the leg of the chair to wake him up. His head snapped up and looked at me. He had his normal face of confusion that would have been followed by incorrectly guessing my name, had I not interrupted the process by telling him to wait for me in the lounge. He reached for a pair of shoes beneath his bed. I don't think he even knew why I was asking him to wait for me, but he asked no questions. Maybe he knew exactly what we were about to do and had no questions... you could never tell with Mr. Rodriguez. He reminded me of an opossum in that regard.

The only people left to round up were Mr. Rash and Mrs. Hawkins, and of course Mrs. Hawkins would be the last. We're always taught to save the best for last, and I was going to need the most time with her. She'd have to get from her bed to her chair, to the elevator, to inside the van. The others could simply take the elevator and wait for me in the parking lot. So with that in mind, I casually strolled to Mr. Rash's room. I was expecting him to be in his usual prickish nature, but I was greeted by something quite different. He was sitting on the edge of his bed watching television. He already had his jacket and shoes on. I could tell he was really ready to go, because he topped the whole outfit off with a red baseball cap. Old men always wear caps when they're going out in public. They're either trying to avoid a sunburn or look younger and less bald. Maybe both.

"You look ready to go," I said from his doorway. He stood up from his bed and turned off the television.

"What did you say?" he asked?

"I said you look ready to go."

"You're right," he said, "I wouldn't miss this for anything in the world." He zipped up his jacket and walked out in the hall. "Where are we going?" he asked.

"To the lounge," I said. "You must really be looking forward to meeting Matlock's dog." As I finished stating my observation, Mr. Rash took his cap off and scratched his head.

"I don't give a rat's ass about Matlock's dog," he said, "I told ya; I'm only coming to watch you mess this thing up." I stared at him with genuine disgust. He was impossible to like, and I had tried. No matter how I approached him, he was a dick. If he weren't at Harrington's, he'd be the old man yelling at kids to stay off his front lawn. "Where's Martha?" he asked.

"She called in sick," I said.

"It's starting already," he laughed. "See you in the lounge, kid." He chuckled and walked away. I bit my lip as I watched Mr. Rash round the corner. I wanted to yell at him. It wasn't in my nature to be laughed at. In a way, that's what this whole plan was about... proving I'm not a joke. Putting up with Mr. Rash's shit was a price I had to pay.

Mrs. Hawkins was next. I wondered where Amanda was. If she wasn't in the room, I could get Mrs. Hawkins dressed and in a wheelchair in under ten minutes. If she was in the room, I may not be able to get Mrs. Hawkins out of there. I wasn't sure what Amanda was up to, but I didn't trust her. I had a feeling that next time I saw her things were going to be ugly. With that thought in mind, I walked into Mrs. Hawkins' room. Luckily, Amanda was nowhere to be seen, so I dressed and placed Mrs. Hawkins in her wheelchair as fast as humanly possible. She may not have had the best outfit on, but she didn't need the best outfit. She could make almost anything outfit look great. Plus, we were going to the park. No sense in her wearing anything too nice to stain.

We left her room and got in an elevator. Harrington's kept the vans in a parking lot beside the building. Staff parked in the rear of the big tan building, guests parked in the front, and the vans were on the side. On Harrington's fourth side was a busy road, Pacific Boulevard. I had to get Mrs. Hawkins in a van and park it in front of Harrington's. Then I had to run upstairs to the second-floor lounge and grab the others. The elevator opened to the ground level. I rolled Mrs. Hawkins to van #6 and turned the engine on. There was a note on the blinker that said the van needed to be serviced. That meant no one would miss it if it was gone, all the more reason to use it for my now unauthorized trip. While it was warming up, I used the hydraulic lift to load Mrs. Hawkins in and buckle her up. Once she was secure, I drove the van to the front of Harrington's. I locked the doors, and left Mrs. Hawkins inside while I went to grab the others. The elevator was in use when I entered the first-floor lobby. I waited and looked around the first floor. It was no wonder everyone wanted to work that floor. The staff barely paid attention to the residents. They talked on cell phones and looked at computers. The residents didn't seem to mind. They watched TV and talked. Some even talked on cell phones themselves. As bad as it sounded, I secretly hoped for an employee on the first floor to die, so I could fill their position.

The elevator dinged and broke my thoughts. I stepped in and pressed the button for the second floor. When the doors opened, I saw Mr. Rodriguez, Mrs. Rodriguez (no relation), Mr. Corbit, and Mr. Rash waiting for me. All of them were seated, except for Mr. Rash. I wondered if he had been standing the whole time.

"Are you guys ready to do this?" I asked, walking out of the elevator. They stood up, slowly, and mumbled to each other. "Where's the excitement everyone?" They gathered themselves and moved toward me.

"What are we doing?" asked Mr. Rodriguez.

"I'm taking you all to meet Matlock's dog, Moose." I waited for that spark in his eye that symbolized recognition. I didn't see it. "You don't remember, Mr. Rodriguez?" I asked. "You were the first person who agreed to go on the trip." He looked at me through squinted eyes.

"Who's all going?" he asked. It appeared Mr. Rodriguez was having one of his bad days, but that was okay. I just needed to get him on the van, then it didn't matter where his mind was at.

"I'll explain it more in the van," I said, pressing the elevator button. Mr. Rodriguez stood quiet and waited for my instructions. That was one of the good things about working with dementia patients; they become more controllable as their disease progresses. It was sad, but necessary to exploit at times. Mr. Corbit stepped forward from the back of the group. The elevator dinged.

"Excuse me?"

"Yes," I said.

"Moose is a dog?" asked Mr. Corbit.

"I told you he was a dog!" I said, staring at him indignantly. "I clearly said Matlock's dog, Moose. What were you expecting?"

He looked at me with a genuine expression of confusion, "I thought you meant his dog friend," he said softly.

"What the hell are you talking about?" I snapped.

He blankly looked at me for a moment then said, "I thought you meant your friend, you know, your *"dog."* You people talk like that nowadays, don't you?" The expression on my face must have been one of sheer shock, for Mr. Corbit quickly tried to smooth things over by uttering, "You know I didn't mean it like that, right?"

I understood what he was trying to say and took no offense to his words. I honestly believed old people should be given the right to say whatever they wanted. No apologies or explanations necessary. It was their reward for living so long but being presented with an opportunity to educate Mr. Corbit proved too tempting.

"You people?" I shrieked. "What the hell does that mean, Mr. Corbit?" He didn't answer. He just stood there with an extremely embarrassed look on his face. Feeling I had taught the lesson I intended to teach, I decided to let Mr. Corbit off the hook with a short speech summarizing the lesson learned.

"You know what Mr. Corbit," I said while resting my hand on his shoulder, "I know what you're trying to say, and guess what? I'm not full black, my mom's white. So I'm even less like the young, black, urban male than you might think." I paused for emphasis. "Just goes to show why you can't assume things about people, Mr. Corbit." I smiled and waited for him to thank me. But he didn't thank me. He just looked confused.

"What is it, Mr. Corbit?" I asked.

He was scratching behind his right ear. "I thought you were Mexican," he said. I put my hands on my hips and tried to exhale the anger in one long breath.

"Get back with the group, Mr. Corbit." He started to turn around but stopped and turned back to me.

"I don't want to meet anyone's dog," he said. "I'd rather stay and play guitar. I'm not going." He turned and walked back toward his room. I called after him, but he didn't even look back to acknowledge my words. That was another benefit of old age; you can change your mind at any moment and not have to explain it to anyone. Why would they? They're old. All they have to do is live as many days as they can.

"Didn't even make it to the van," Mr. Rash mocked. I wanted to respond, but his mocking reminded me that Mrs. Hawkins was locked in a van in the parking lot. I had to act quickly, and the trip was officially canceled with only four participants.

"Does anyone else not want to go on the trip?" I asked.

"Where are we going?" asked Mr. Rodriguez. I took that to be my trip's concession speech.

"We're not going anywhere, Mr. Rodriguez. Sorry to get you guys excited for nothing," I said. "Why don't you all go in the cafeteria and be first in line for lunch. Mr. Rodriguez shuffled off. Mrs. Rodriguez, who I doubt understood half of what I had said, followed behind him. Only Mr. Rash remained.

"What's your problem with me?" I asked him. He smiled and took off his red baseball cap.

"I don't have any problem with you," he said. "Hell, you're good entertainment." He quietly laughed to himself. "I told you that Corbit's a real asshole" he added. "Let me get back at him for you."

I looked at him in disbelief. "And how are you going to do that?" I asked.

"Give me your guitar," he responded.

"What? How is giving you my guitar going to get back at Mr. Corbit?" I asked. "And why do you have such a problem with him anyway?"

Mr. Rash slowly put his baseball cap back on, pulling it down snug over his forehead. "Let's just say Donald Corbit gets under my skin, alright?" He lifted his head up and peered at me from under the cap's bill. "Does it matter why Corbit and I don't get along?" he asked. "Not really. All that matters is that he ruined your trip today."

"And how does me giving you my guitar get him back?" I asked slowly.

Apparently annoyed, Mr. Rash explained that Mr. Corbit had been strutting around the nursing home with his guitar, acting like "hot shit" as Mr. Rash put it. From his story, I gathered that the final straw was when Mr. Corbit tried to serenade a certain geriatric named, Mrs. Iris Galdine. Apparently, Mr. Rash had an eye for Iris, and didn't appreciate Mr. Corbit playing guitar for her. Therefore, he needed my guitar so that he could serenade Mrs. Galdine on his own, not to mention, take the wind out of Mr. Corbit's sails. He couldn't act like "hot shit" if he wasn't the only one with a guitar at the nursing home. That was his plan. If Mrs. Hawkins hadn't been stuck in a van downstairs, I would have tripped Mr. Rash and stomped on his old brittle bones. I never understood people who are mean for no reason. What a waste of life. I told him I'd have to think about it, as politely as I could, and left his presence.

I stepped back in the elevator and tried to figure out what to do next. I still had Mrs. Hawkins in my possession, and Rachel was still expecting me at the park. I pushed the elevator button once more. When it opened, Amanda was standing inside. "Shit!" I thought to myself, while trying to act casual.

"What's up, Manders?"

"Looks like your little field trip has fallen apart," she said, "can't say I'm sad to hear it." I stood momentarily speechless trying to figure out how she knew the trip was canceled. I stepped into the elevator.

"It's no big deal," I said, shrugging my shoulders. "Something better's come up anyway."

"Really?" she asked in an unconvinced tone.

"Yea, really!" I mocked in a condescending tone.

"Where's Mrs. Hawkins?" she asked.

"Amanda, what's your deal with her, huh? You're so protective of her… it's a little creepy." The elevator doors closed and I pressed the button for the lobby.

"I'll tell you what my deal is." She paused for an unnatural moment before speaking again. "Mrs. Hawkins is my great aunt," she finally said. "At first, I was only working here as part of my nursing program at the college, but I stayed here to protect her from you, because you know what *"creeps me out,"* the fact that you like to watch me and Ruben bathe her!"

"I like to believe Mrs. Hawkins enjoys my presence," I interjected as respectfully as possible.

"What's wrong with you? She's 85 years old!" Amanda's face was starting to redden. She glared at me and tucked a strip of red hair behind her left ear.

"Actually, she's 83 years old," I said politely as possible.

"Whatever! I've told management about your behavior," she said, "so watch your step." She folded her arms in front of her, cocked her head to one side, and smiled proudly. The elevator dinged as it arrived in the lobby.

"Listen, Manders, I'd love to keep chatting, but I have a date to get to." I paused and reached for my cell phone. The elevator doors opened behind me. "You'll have to excuse me, I'm a little busy," I said while pretending to peruse my phone for important information. I placed the phone to my ear and started a fake phone call when Amanda spoke.

"It's barely 10:30 in the morning, and you're at work, you don't have any date to get to," she said. "Now where's Mrs. Hawkins?" I shook my head slowly from side to side.

"I don't know where she is," I said, "but if she's anything like me, she wanted to get far away from you." Feeling fairly proud of my witty comment, I turned my back on her and headed across the lobby, holding an imaginary conversation the whole time. I breathed easier when I heard the elevator doors ding and close again.

To my lack of surprise, Mrs. Hawkins was sitting exactly where I had left her. I unlocked the door and climbed in. Before I turned the ignition on, I looked at Mrs. Hawkins in disbelief. How could someone as great as her be related to Amanda? Amanda was skinny, with long reddish, auburn hair and rosy cheeks. Even at twenty-something she looked like a thirteen-year-old girl who had aged badly. Mrs. Hawkins looked like she was a curvy vivacious thing in her youth. A brunette firecracker. She looked like a woman who had broken a few hearts in her lifetime. The kind of woman your wife hates the minute she meets her. Amanda was proof of how watered-down genes could become.

I started the van and pulled out of the parking lot. As I turned onto Pacific Boulevard, I saw Amanda in my rear-view mirror running toward the van with her arms waving. I had had my fill of her already. Besides, all she was going to do was try to stop me from taking Mrs. Hawkins to meet Moose, or whatever I was now taking her to do. I turned right quickly and accelerated out of the parking lot. I looked for a mud puddle I could splash Amanda with on my way out, but there weren't any. It hadn't rained in over a week. Once on the road, I had to figure out my next move. Rachel would be at the park in about an hour, and I still had to stop by my house and grab Moose. I decided to use the van as homebase. I'd grab Moose and kill an hour in the van, then meet Rachel at the park. I didn't know what Amanda wanted, but I was sure my speeding off hadn't helped the situation any. Therefore, I couldn't hang at the house; I'd be a sitting duck.

SUNDAY 11:04 A.M.

I parked in my driveway and ran inside. Moose was lying on the couch. I let him out in the backyard and let him do his business. I was in a hurry, but I sure as hell wasn't going to pick up after him at the park. After about five minutes, Moose had finished his dance and walked back to the door. I placed his leash on him and led him to the van. He sat up front with me. We backed out of the driveway and hit the road again. The whole process couldn't have taken more than ten minutes.

We drove around downtown a little while before I parked in a grocery store parking lot. I took my cell phone out and texted Rachel. I asked her if she was still meeting me at the park. She replied she was and would be there around noon. That meant I had around forty-six minutes to burn before heading to Bryant Park. What was I going to do with a hundred- and fifty-pound dog and an 83-year-old woman for forty-six minutes? I needed somewhere that would be comfortable for all of us. I was stressed, but luckily, I didn't have to think hard. The answer to my question came to me like a snail to a puddle of beer- the skate park. Moose could lie in the grass, I could smoke some grass, and Mrs. Hawkins could get some fresh air. It would calm all of us down. I put the van in drive and headed for the skate park.

One nice thing about skateboarders is their reliability. At no other park in town could you guarantee that people would be there, no matter what time it was. Some parks were busy with evening basketball players. Other parks were busy with seniors playing bocce ball. Only the skate park was consistently filled with poorly dressed 12-to-30-year-olds skipping school, missing work, or simply wasting their lives. This day was no different. I parked the van in the rear of the parking lot, in hopes of not being spotted, and activated the hydraulic lift for Mrs. Hawkins. Moose whined while he waited to be let out. Once Mrs. Hawkins was out of the van, I opened the passenger door and let Moose out. I tied the end of his leash to the front of Mrs. Hawkins' wheelchair, that way I'd have both hands free to push her, and Moose would do half the work for me.

When we reached the skateboarders, they were doing their usual acrobatics. I was impressed that these kids could not only do such complicated aerial stunts but could do them at 11 in the morning. I freed Moose from the wheelchair and tied him to a nearby tree. I parked Mrs. Hawkins under a shade tree and walked toward the skaters and their friends. Curious does not describe the facial expressions I received as I made my way across the grass.

"Dude, is that your mom?" a blonde-haired kid asked as I glanced back over my shoulder.

"Who? Her?" I asked, pretending to be confused. "No, she's just an old lady I'm paid to take care of." I waited for the kid's suspicion to subside. "So what're you guys doing?"

"Just skating." He was studying me.

I was looking for the red-headed kid I smoked with the last time I was there. He wasn't anywhere to be found. Or maybe he was there? I couldn't tell, they all looked the same to me.

"Are you a narc, dude?" the blonde-haired kid asked me.

"A narc? What? No." I laughed at his question in an attempt to quell his fears. There were a few more kids around him now; the oldest couldn't have been more than twenty-three. I reiterated my non-narcness.

"No," I said, "I'm not a narc at all, but it's funny you ask." I looked around before I continued. "I actually did come here to score a little pot from you guys. Maybe I could trade you a few beers for it?" They exchanged glances.

"It's not even noon yet, dude" a chubby kid on my right said.

"I know it's early, but I figured you wouldn't want me mooching off you, so I thought we-"

"NARC!" a voice interrupted. I tried to locate the face but failed.

"I'm not a narc," I began.

"Prove it!" a girl yelled from the rear of the group.

"How do I prove I'm not a narc?" I asked.

"Easy." The blonde-haired kid said. "We'll get you high, but you've got to share it with your mom back there." I turned and looked at Mrs. Hawkins.

"First off, she's not my mom. Second off, how do I share it with her? She's over 80 years-old and partially paralyzed."

"Just blow it in her ear," he replied.

"What? That'll get her high?"

"Yeah, blow it in her ear. That'll totally get her high." I skeptically looked at him. "Haven't you ever gotten a dog high before?" he asked. I didn't have to pause to think about it. I had never gotten Moose high. Never had a desire to.

"Blowing weed smoke in that old lady's ear will prove to you I'm not a narc?" I asked.

"Among other things," he replied as his friends laughed. I debated what to do. Moose was laying in the shade sniffing the ground. He looked like he could survive a couple of minutes without my attention. I changed my focus from him to Mrs. Hawkins. She was sitting motionless in her chair. "Maybe a little reefer would liven her up," I said to myself.

"How many hits do I have to blow in her ear?" I asked. What's it take, like two or three earfuls of smoke to get someone high?" They had a quick discussion among themselves before someone said three hits sounded about right.

The skinny blonde kid called for a girl named Sarah, and a manly looking girl came up from the edge of the group. She also had blonde hair, but her upper body was muscular and hunched over. I wondered if they were boyfriend and girlfriend. I hoped not, because I didn't find her attractive at all. He could have done better. It's usually the girl who settles when choosing a partner. She took a sandwich bag of marijuana out of a green backpack and handed it to the skinny blonde boy. He took the bag to a park bench, where he rolled something they called a blunt. I had never smoked a blunt, but it appeared to be nothing more than a cigar emptied of its tobacco and replaced with weed. It seemed a bit excessive to me. I looked back over at Mrs. Hawkins and wondered if she had ever smoked weed before. Even though she couldn't talk, I had always pictured her as a party girl in her youth, therefore, I was sure she had smoked weed once in her life. Deciding that to be a good enough reason to get her high again, I accepted the skater's challenge.

"So it's just three hits?" I said while the blonde kid finished rolling the marijuana cigar.

"That's right," he said, "just three hits of this Alaskan Thunderfuck in one of her ears. After that, we'll all know you're not a narc, and you can buy us some beer." He started licking and rolling the cigar. I had suspicion that I was being played a fool in this exchange, but I really needed to get high. I had a lot of pressure on my shoulders: I had to impress Rachel with Mrs. Hawkins, I had to keep control of Moose, and above all else; I had Mrs. Hawkins welfare in my hands. I'm sure she was a little stressed over the day's events. Maybe an earful of weed smoke was just what she needed? Help relax her a little. Put her at ease. The blonde kid got up from the bench and walked toward me.

"You ready to do this?" he asked while waving the blunt in front of his face. It suddenly felt like I was in high school again. Here I was about to do something I not only knew was wrong, but honestly objected to, all in an effort to prove something to some pimple-faced kid. I felt like an idiot, but I couldn't back out now.

We walked toward Mrs. Hawkins and formed a circle around her. She was slumped forward in her chair.

"Are you sure no one is going to see us?" I asked.

"We've got you covered, dude," the blond kid said while handing me the blunt and a lighter. "Just light it up, blow it in her ear, take a few tokes for yourself, and pass it back to me. That's all there is to it, dude." He stood watching me. The whole circle of eyes was on me.

I put the blunt in my mouth, lit the other end, and inhaled. The weed tasted harsh, like tobacco, and hurt my lungs. I must have taken too big of a hit because I coughed and blew smoke and spit all over. The group of skaters laughed and made fun of me. After regaining my breath, I took a smaller dose and held it in. Kneeling on one knee, I placed my mouth next to Mrs. Hawkins' ear and gently blew my hit into it. The smoke bounced off the side of her head and burned my eyes. When I finished, I leaned back and looked at Mrs. Hawkins face. Her expression was the same as it always was, only her eyes blinked faster than usual.

"Give her another one, except get closer this time," a voice in the background said. I didn't even try to locate the face. Again I put the cigar in my mouth and drew in smoke. It still hurt my throat, but before I had finished inhaling, my mind became fuzzy and my eyelids drooped to half-mast.

I leaned in once more toward Mrs. Hawkins' ear. Getting as close as possible to her ear, without actually kissing it, I shot a stream of solid smoke into her ear canal. As I finished, her head twitched from side to side a little. I doubt the skateboard kids noticed it, but it was the most voluntary movement I had seen from her. Maybe this stuff was good for her. The skaters all laughed and recorded the event on their cell phones. I took another hit for myself and passed the weed cigar back to the blonde kid.

"Some good stuff, huh?" he asked. I nodded silently in agreement. "We've got a whole lot of this shit," he said proudly as he showed me two large zip lock bags inside the green backpack. They passed the blunt around for a few minutes while I spaced out and stared at the ground. Moose's bark broke my concentration. The skaters turned their heads in every direction, trying to figure out what Moose was barking at.

The answer was on the opposite side of the park, a police officer was walking towards us. I could barely see him because I was surrounded by the kids. The blonde-haired kid became visibly nervous and called for the mannish blonde girl. They talked quietly and quickly about something, but I paid little attention, I was too high to really listen. Plus, I had fears of my own. All I could think of was Amanda! I knew she had called the cops on me for taking Mrs. Hawkins out of Harrington's. She was so predictable! I thought about running, but again, I was too high. The skaters on the other hand, were not.

In all directions they broke out in dead sprints. Some hopped on their skateboards and fled. The blonde kid flicked the blunt in the bushes, threw the green backpack onto Mrs. Hawkins lap, and ran away. I watched all the commotion around me in a fog of slow motion. Moose slobbered and barked at the kids who ran past him. Mrs. Hawkins sat slumped forward in her wheelchair with a backpack full of marijuana on her lap. She gently bobbed her head back and forth.

The police officer spoke into a walkie-talkie on his shoulder and approached me at a gallop.

"Everything alright?" he asked. I paused, unsure of what he meant.

"Um, yeah, everything's okay," I responded.

"Those kids bother guests at this park all the time. We've been trying to protect people like you and this elderly woman from their raucous behavior."

"Uhh… thank you," I said slowly.

"No problem," he said before talking into his walkie-talkie some more. "What's in the bag?" he asked, pointing at the backpack on Mrs. Hawkins' lap. I instantly became nervous and swallowed hard.

"It's just her emergency items," I lied. "You know, medications, first aid kit, that kind of stuff."

"Right," he said, studying her closely. "Is she okay?"

"What? Of course she's okay. She's fine." I looked at Mrs. Hawkins and saw a string of drool running from her mouth.

"You got a napkin in that backpack?" the officer asked.

"Oh, I don't need a napkin for a little drool," I said, whipping the saliva from Mrs. Hawkins' lip. "It's a labor of love really," I continued. The officer gave me a strange look before asking if I "needed any help with anything?" Again, I was slow-witted from the weed, so my reaction was slow. I was going to tell him everything was fine, and I didn't need his help with anything, but before I spoke, I saw the blonde kid hiding behind a bush in the distance. He, no doubt, wanted his weed back. Now, normally I wouldn't be the type to lie, but I felt degraded by his actions before; that little prick made me blow smoke into an 83-year-old woman's ear!

Seeing the opportunity that was presenting itself to me, I quickly sobered up, and milked it to its fullest. I had the officer help me load Moose and Mrs. Hawkins into the van. I put the backpack under Mrs. Hawkins lap blanket and placed it in the front seat. I couldn't believe he didn't smell it. He assisted Mrs. Hawkins onto the van's lift, then he politely closed the door behind her. I thanked him verbally for his help with Mrs. Hawkins and Moose, and silently for helping me rob an 18-year-old douchebag. It's funny how talking to a cop can make you forget you're inebriated.

SUNDAY 12:13 P.M.

After starting the engine, my phone rang. It was Rachel. She was already waiting for me at Bryant Park. I was late. That was another thing she liked about Sean. He was on time. He bought her things. He was more considerate, overall, than I was. I hung up with her and started the van. I could smell the weed in the backpack in the seat beside me. It was either really good stuff, or there was simply a large amount of it, or perhaps both. As I got ready to leave the park, I noticed Toucan staring at me from the sidewalk. He looked as if he was trying to determine if it was in fact me he was looking at. I wondered if he was confused because he had never seen me outside of the bar, or because his mind was so wasted that he couldn't remember who I was. After he decided he did indeed recognize me, he walked toward the van. Normally I would have driven away from him, like I did Amanda earlier, but I was still stoned and my motor skills were delayed as a result. He approached the van with salutations.

"What's up, man?" he asked in his perpetually wasted drawl. "Don't see you around here often," he continued. "And why was there a cop by your van, man?" I laughed a little at his behavior. He was obviously sketched out about what he had seen.

"It was nothing like that," I said. "He was just helping me load Mrs. Hawkins here. Came down here to get the crew some fresh air," I said motioning to Moose and Mrs. Hawkins. Toucan peered inside the van with a surprisingly intense focus.

"Is that your dog, man?" he asked. "That's a pretty dog."

I rubbed Moose's on the head. "Yep," I said, "this is my dog, Moose."

Toucan stared at Moose and bobbed his head up and down. "That's a pretty dog right there."

"Thank you." I said.

"Is he a good dog?" Toucan asked. "He looks like a good dog."

"Yeah, he's a good dog, Toucan."

A smile struck Toucan's lips as he spoke. "I could tell he's a good dog. Yep, a dog like that you've got to pet every day!"

His comment caught me off guard. "What?" I asked.

Toucan stopped staring at Moose and looked at me. "You gotta pet that kind of dog every day," he said straight faced.

"As opposed to what other kind of dog, Toucan?" I asked. Obviously confused, he scrunched his eyebrow and contorted his mouth into shapes that made you think he was going to speak, but nothing came out. "What I'm saying is, what kind of dog don't you have to pet every...you know what, I don't have time for this, Toucan!" He was beginning to frustrate me. "I'm late," I said. "I need to get somewhere." I buckled my seat belt and looked back at Toucan. He was no longer staring at Moose, nor was he looking at me. He was focused on Mrs. Hawkins.

"Is she dead, man?" he asked.

"What? No, she's not dead, she's sleeping." I suddenly found myself feeling defensive. What are you doing down here?" I asked.

"Oh, I'm always here, man. This is where you come to score the good stuff, bro." He was now resting his forearm on the van's door. I wanted him to leave, and I was about to tell him as much, but he asked me a question that shifted my focus.

"What's that smell, man?" He was trying to stick his nose through my window.

"What's it smell like?" I asked scared as to what he might say.

"Smells like the kill," he responded. "Did you grab some of the goods or what, bro?" I didn't know how to respond. I couldn't let Toucan know I had a backpack full of marijuana, or he wouldn't leave me alone. I also couldn't let him know I had no idea the value or quantity of the weed in the backpack. If I exposed my ignorance, I'd never get the full value of what I had in my possession. And that was important if I tried to sell it to him or anyone else. It was now a matter of marketing. I decided to use Toucan's expertise to my advantage.

"Yeah, I picked up a little somethin'," I said, trying to sound cool. I'm worried I got ripped off though. How much do you usually pay for the stuff?" I asked.

"Depends on how much you buy," he responded. "An eighth is usually fifty bucks."

"How much is an eighth?" I asked. He looked at me in shock.

"You haven't been smoking long, have you?" he asked with his eyebrows raised. He then went on to explain that an eighth is fifty dollars, and supposedly weighs 3.5 grams, but is usually less so a dealer has more weed to sell, and essentially makes more money off less product. He then went on to tell me how marijuana is a natural substance and only God can truly say whether something's illegal or not. And for the finale of his weed sermon, he reminded me that the constitution was written on hemp, touted the superior quality of hemp ropes, and informed me that at one time it was illegal in America for people possessing hemp seeds *not* to plant them.

I disregarded most of his stoner trivia and imagined how much money the blonde kid had tossed onto Mrs. Hawkins' lap. If 3.5 grams was an eighth, and an eighth went for fifty-bucks, then I had a pretty penny sitting in the backseat.

Interrupting Toucan and his Jeopardy-like knowledge of cannabis, I told him I had just purchased a large amount, and if he wanted any, he could meet me at Lumpy's later to discuss business. I started pulling the van forward, forcing him to stop leaning on my driver side door.

"What time are you going to Lumpy's?" he asked as I pulled into the street.

"Does it really matter?" I replied, "You're there at all hours anyway." I waved goodbye and accelerated out of the parking lot.

I headed to Walmart. I had to buy a scale. If I was gonna try to sell weed, I had to know how much I had in the backpack. That way, I could make an educated guess as to how much to charge. And I thought selling drugs was for people who *didn't* want to work for a living or use high school algebra. I suddenly respected drug dealers a little more.

I parked in front of the Walmart superstore. This place was huge! And much like the skate park, it was always packed, no matter what time of day you went. I cracked all of the windows for both Moose and Mrs. Hawkins (no sense in one of them overheating because I played favorites). Before exiting the van, I sent Rachel a text telling her something had come up, and that I'd be at Bryant Park in about half an hour. Even though the day had provided me with unforeseen events, that was no reason to be tardy or leave someone waiting.

I went inside Walmart and asked a heavy-set man where I could find the scales. He directed me to the bathroom scales. I found him again and asked where I could find the other type of scales.

"What type of scale are you looking for?" he asked suspiciously. I quickly spurted off the first lie that came to mind.

"I'm a cook, you see, and I've got a big dinner party coming over soon, so I need a scale to measure ingredients to the smallest decimal. I'd prefer an electronic scale, but an old-fashioned triple-beam scale would work fine also." He looked at me and folded his arms across his chest.

"We sell those types of scales, but they're kept in a glass case on aisle eleven, got tired of teenagers trying to steal them." He studied me while he waited for my response. I stood uncomfortably in front of him and pondered a way out.

"You said aisle eleven, right?"

"Yep."

"Okay, well thanks for your help," I said, turning away.

"You got some green vegetables to weigh?" he asked. I stopped and turned back around.

"Yeah... I'll probably be using some broccoli or-"

"Cut the shit." He said flatly. "I know what you want the scale for."

"I told you, I'm a cook, and I've got some people coming over."

"Right," he said, smirking at me. "Look, I know it's hard to tell who you can trust, and who you can't, but I'm not a narc, and I'd love to buy some of what you're about to weigh."

I didn't know what to say. In a matter of minutes I had gone from retirement facility worker to major drug dealer. It was an effortless transition. No wonder people get mixed up in this line of work. Remembering that I already had Toucan lined up to meet me later, I gave the Walmart employee the same directions. He told me he got off at six, and that he'd drive to the bank, then go straight to

Lumpy's. He tried to tell me how he's been out of good smoke for a while now, and how desperately he wanted to find a new "hook up." I listened to him and secretly wondered why all potheads tend to be blabbermouths, first Toucan, now this guy. It didn't help that my mind was still cloudy after the skaters made me…"Oh shit!" I thought, "Mrs. Hawkins is still in the van." I caught his cliquey short and told him I'd see him at Lumpy's after six.

On my way out of Walmart, Rachel called me again. She was still waiting for me at Bryant Park.

"You come or not?" she asked.

"I'm on my way, I replied. Traffic is awful. I'll be there in less than ten minutes."

"Hurry up!" she demanded. "I not wait any longer." I hung up with her and walked to the van. Moose was in the back of the van licking Mrs. Hawkins' face. There was a skinny, middle-aged woman reaching in the window of the van's passenger door.

"Can I help you?" I asked.

"Is this your van?" she angrily asked.

"Yea," I said, "why?"

"Because that woman is trapped inside a hot car! That can't be good for her health! She looks dead, for God's sake!"

"She's not dead!" I yelled. "She's fine. I was only inside for few a minutes, so mind your own goddamn business!" The woman stood in shock with her mouth open. She clutched her purse in front of her and watched me get in the van. Before I got out of ear shot, I heard her yell what a terrible person I was, and how I was going to hell. I found her words ironic because I felt the same way about her.

SUNDAY 12:47 P.M.

It was a pleasant surprise to see Rachel waiting for me at the park. I assumed she would have left already and this whole field trip would have been a complete waste of time and energy. She was sitting on the hood of a silver car. It looked like a Camaro, or something similar. It had to be Sean's because I sure as hell didn't buy her a sports car. The last thing I saw her driving was my old tan Toyota Camry. It appeared she was already reaping the advantages of living with Sean. If I was going to convince her to return to me, I had to impress her with Mrs. Hawkins and Moose. It wasn't going to be easy, but nothing worth having ever is. She was going to be wowed by my control over Mrs. Hawkins. She was going to be impressed by the fact Harrington's had given me permission to embark on such a field trip. And lastly, she was going to see that I actually did have leader characteristics. That spark would return to her eye, and she would follow me home. Hell, maybe we'd just use the backseat of Sean's Camaro? Either way, the point was, she was gonna want me back. And that's when the real plan would fall into place. Once she moved back in with me, returned Sean's house keys, and unpacked her belongings, I'd hug her close, kiss her neck, and whisper softly in her ear, "I'm so glad you're back. However, I think we need to take some space. I want you out by tomorrow evening." It was gonna happen, and it all began now.

I stepped out of the van and unloaded Moose. I activated the wheelchair lift and waited for Mrs. Hawkins. Rachel walked toward me and waved while she talked on her phone. When Mrs. Hawkins was ready to roll, I once again tied Moose to the front of her chair and walked to meet Rachel. He became excited at seeing her and ran to meet her. He got about two feet before the leash jerked him around the neck. The recoil lifted him off the ground and threw him backwards. The force of the whole event tossed Mrs. Hawkins forward and out of the wheelchair. In the most slow-motion fall I had ever seen, or could ever even try to explain, Mrs. Hawkins tumbled forward in a heap. She landed face first on the pavement. I picked her up as fast as I could and was relieved when I saw her forehead had taken the brunt of the fall. She had a nasty scrape above her eyebrows that was beginning to bleed. Rachel was staring at me in shock. She said goodbye to whoever she was talking to and put the phone in her purse.

"Who you talking to? Sean?" I asked trying my best to pretend Mrs. Hawkins had not just fallen on her face.

"Don't matter who I talk to," she answered. "Who that?" she asked pointing at Mrs. Hawkins.

"This is Mrs. Hawkins," I responded. "She's the woman I'm taking out today." I paused and waited for Rachel's reaction. There was none. "They don't let us take the residents out too often," I continued, "You have to be an important person to get that type of treatment, you know?" I patted Mrs. Hawkins' shoulder and glanced down at her. Besides the blood running down her forehead, she was drooling again. Her head was drooping down into her chest. I looked for something to wipe her slobber with. I wasn't touching the blood.

"She dead?" she asked.

"Why does everyone keep saying that? No, she's not dead! I'm taking her out because I'm in a new management position at Harrington's. I probably make as much as Sean does now."

"I thought you were bringing group of people to park. You said you leader now. And why Moose here?" I instinctively petted Moose and looked at her in amazement. She really wasn't the same Rachel I had known. Gone was the quiet woman I had boated over from Vietnam (because I couldn't afford a plane) and forced to love me. She was different now. She had changed. All I could think when she was talking to me was, "Why was she being such a bitch?" Who did she think she was?" I stopped petting Moose and jumped into another lie.

"Well, actually, Jiop Lin," I began, "Moose is here because many studies have shown that pets can extend the lives of old people.

That's why I'm taking Mrs. Hawkins out to test the new program I created." Rachel looked at me with mild curiosity.

"Maybe you try program with someone younger," she said. "I think this lady dead already." Besides the fact it was one of the better grammatical sentences I had ever heard Rachel speak, I was again struck by her newfound spunk. Through the course of our separation, Rachel had shown herself to be a witty bitch with a devilish streak of sarcasm. I wish she would have shown that side of her personality earlier, it might have prompted me to work harder on our relationship and kept me from cheating on her. It kind of made me want her back. She was behaving like a feminine me. Too bad I had already decided to dump her in an attempt to permanently ruin her life. It's funny how relationships work in cycles.

"She's not dead at all," I said, again resting my hand on Mrs. Hawkins's shoulder. "You've still got plenty of life to live don't you Mrs. Hawkins?" I looked down at her half expecting a response to my rhetorical question. She didn't say a thing. She was again sitting slumped forward with her head hanging down. There was a small pool of blood starting to gather on the blanket covering her lap. I became a little worried about her health. "Maybe I should get her home?" I said out loud.

Rachel chewed her gum loudly and repeatedly checked her phone. I was about to lose her. She was not a very patient woman. That was the first American trait she acquired.

"I need go," she said after checking her phone again.

"Where are you in such a hurry to?" I asked. "Don't you want to hear about all the things that have happened with me since you left?"

"Nothing new wit you," she remarked. "You still clean old people; Moose still stink, and Sean still leader. I have go now. This big waste my time." I was in a tough spot; I needed to get Mrs. Hawkins somewhere safe to clean her wound, Moose was getting tired of sitting, and Rachel wanted to leave. I only had one choice left, come clean and tell her the truth.

"Wait a second, Rachel, don't leave yet." I pushed Mrs. Hawkins and Moose to a bench and motioned for Rachel to come sit by me. She reluctantly agreed. She walked toward the bench I was on with small strides. She had short legs, but they were beautifully shaped- thin ankles, athletic calves, and sinuous thighs. She was wearing a white sundress that was almost see-through when the sun hit it just right. A woman in a see-through dress is sexy by itself, but add the fact that Rachel seldom wore underwear, and you have every man's dream! I tried to catch a peak on her way toward me, but there wasn't enough sun on her dress. She sat on my left, and I grabbed her hand.

"Rachel, I have to be honest with you. I only wanted you to come down here today so you could see me in charge of my environment, find that attractive, and move back in with me. I know

I can't give you all the material things Sean does, but I can give you one thing he can't: true love. I've loved you ever since you got off that boat. Shit, I loved you before that. It was your picture on the website that made me fall in love with you. Yep, the minute I saw your picture I knew we were meant to be together, that's why I emptied my savings to buy you. I think we can make it work." (I paused for effect.) "So, why don't you just call Sean and tell him you're going home?" I kissed her hand and hugged her tight as the closing statement of my speech. Rachel had indeed changed some over time, but she would have to be a completely different woman not to fall for that speech. The Rachel I knew was a sucker for declarations of love. I smiled a little and waited for her response. After what felt like five or six minutes, she finally spoke.

"You sure she not dead?" she asked. Before I could gather myself to respond, she continued. "Maybe take her to doctor." She took her phone out of her pocket again and said, "I'm go now. You still loser." She patted me on the arm and started to walk away.

"Wait a minute, Rachel! That's it? You're done, just like that?" She closed her phone and smiled at me.

"I outgrow you," she said in a soft tone. "Sean better for me. I hope we still be friends." She grabbed my arm again, but this time she rubbed it gently. I was again amazed with her breakup skills. Not only had she mastered the speech, save for the grammar aspect of it, but she had even involved supportive physical contact. The gentle rubbing of my arm actually did make me feel a little better. She had to be getting breakup advice from someone. However, I pulled away from her and came back to my senses.

"How did you outgrow me?" I asked incredulously. "You wouldn't even be here if it wasn't for me! I'm the one who brought you to this country! Have you already forgotten that?"

"How could I forget eight-day boat ride?" she asked.

"So this *is* about the boat. Rachel, I told you I couldn't afford a plane ticket. I did the best I could."

"There was rats on boat!" she interrupted. "I scared I get scurvy!" My jaw dropped in response.

"Where'd you learn the word scurvy?" I asked.

"It not matter," she shrieked, "I with Sean now! We done. Have good life cleaning old dead people." She turned and walked away. Even though I tried to tell myself otherwise, I knew that was the end of Jiop Lin and me. She didn't go back and forth once she made a decision. Everything with her was final. Well, everything except her marriage to me that is.

"Bitch," I muttered as I watched her walk away. I turned around and looked at Moose and Mrs. Hawkins. "Now what?" I said to myself. Moose was starting to drool, an obvious sign he needed water, and Mrs. Hawkins was still leaking blood from her forehead. I had to leave the park, but I couldn't go back to Harrington's. Amanda was no doubt waiting for my return. I had luckily escaped one cop already; I didn't see the point in pressing my luck. Amanda had, no doubt, put an A.P.B. out on Mrs. Hawkins whereabouts. If I returned her in good health I'd surely be arrested, so returning her with a divot of forehead missing was probably not in my best interest. As I sat on the bench pondering what to do next, I remembered I was sitting on a large stash of pot that could possibly help me find a way out of this mess. It was 1:15pm. There was nearly five hours before I needed to meet Toucan and the Walmart guy at Lumpy's. I needed entertainment.

SUNDAY 1:32 P.M.

After soaking up as much of Mrs. Hawkins' blood as her lap blanket would allow, I loaded everyone back into the van. I checked Mrs. Hawkins' pulse as I rolled her onto the chairlift. She was alive alright, but her pulse was faint. Once everyone was safely secured in the van, I drove downtown. Perhaps it was the lingering effects of the weed, but I decided it best to head to Lumpy's early. I could get water for Moose, get Mrs. Hawkins out of the sun, while waiting for my customers, Toucan and the Walmart dude, to come purchase the pot from me. The last thing I needed with Mrs. Hawkins being injured and Moose dehydrating was a bag of narcotics in my possession. However, I was almost certain the cash from the deal would help me out of this situation somehow.

I parked the van three blocks from Lumpy's in a shitty part of downtown. Before leaving the van to its imminent theft or stripping, I weighed the contents of the green backpack. It took longer than I thought it would, and it was hot in the van with its windows rolled up. Sweat was running down my face and back. I didn't have any plastic bags, so I used Mrs. Hawkins' socks as containers. I would have used my socks, but like I said, I was sweaty. Mrs. Hawkins' feet never sweated. She couldn't even move enough to work up a sweat.

The big plastic bag inside the backpack held a little less than two ounces. That meant, if I remembered Toucan's pot to cash ratio correctly, I had close to 16 eighths, and if one eighth cost $50, then I had around $800 worth of weed in Mrs. Hawkins' lap. I stuffed Mrs. Hawkins' socks each with an ounce and tied knots at the top of them. Stuffing the socks into my pockets, I locked the van's doors and headed toward Lumpy's with Moose and Mrs. Hawkins. As we approached the bar, I looked at the wound on Mrs. Hawkins' forehead. Then I looked up and saw a green Toyota corolla parked in front of Lumpy's. I was instantly struck with two conflicting emotions; 1. The good news was Mrs. Hawkins head had finally stopped bleeding and 2. The bad news was Garrett was bartending today.

SUNDAY 1:55 P.M.

Garrett was a dick in his early thirties. He was around the same age I was, but he still acted like the cool jock in high school. The reason that bothered me so badly was because the tables had obviously turned on Garrett, but he was too stupid to recognize or admit it. I'm sure in high school he was the big, manly senior who tormented the geeks, dated all the hot freshman girls, but now he waited on the same kids he picked on in high school. The joke was on him. Instead of recognizing the failure his life had become, Garrett walked around with an air of superiority about him. All the patrons hated him. He had slicked black hair and a smoothly shaven face, except for a patch of hair at the bottom of his lower lip he like to call a "soul patch." He wore jeans with holes in them, and clean shirts two sizes too small. He was everything you hated to see in a local pub. Local pubs are for communal losers to meet, mingle, and hopefully get lucky with one another. It's these types of activities that give dirty backwater towns their charm. No one goes to a bar like Lumpy's to be noticed. No one tries to impress anyone else with their clothes, money, or status. Lumpy's is a place to help you forget all those things about yourself, because chances are, you're not too proud of any of them. But simply sliding in and getting drunk in solitude is difficult when Garrett's serving the swill. I tried to enter as inconspicuously as possible.

"What in the hell do you think you're doing?" Garrett asked as I guided Moose and Mrs. Hawkins through the door. He had the classic bartender towel over his shoulder. "What a douche!" I thought to myself.

"I'm just trying to get a drink, Garrett." I pushed Mrs. Hawkins to a table and told Moose to sit.

"You can't bring a dog into the bar, buddy." I looked back at Moose as if shocked to see him there.

"Did I bring a dog in here?" I asked out loud. "My bad, just let me get a few drinks and I'll be out of here." Garrett smiled at me and shook his head slowly before he spoke.

"I'm not letting you drink shit, so get your old ass grandma and your dirty ass dog out of here!" He laughed and smiled with the drunks at the bar.

"You're a real asshole, Garrett," I said while maneuvering Mrs. Hawkins across the room.

"What'd you say to me?" Garrett asked

"I said you're an asshole and all your shirts are way, way too small. I mean seriously, you look like you're wearing your little brother's clothes. Grow up." I opened the door and backed Mrs. Hawkins out. Before the door closed, I heard Garrett say something about kicking my ass the next time he saw me. He even talked trash like a high school jock. After I let the door slam, I turned and saw Toucan walking toward me. He waved and sped up his pace.

"What's up, man?" he asked. "You're just the guy I was looking for. Do you still have the stuff to sell?" He was petting Moose and talking puppy talk to him.

"Yeah, I've still got the stuff, Toucan, it's $400 an ounce." He stopped petting Moose and looked up at me in amazement.

"I ain't got that much money. I only..." he trailed off. "Is she okay?" he asked, pointing at Mrs. Hawkins.

"She's fine!" I blurted. "Now how much money do you have?"

"I only have a hundred dollars," he said. He shrugged and petted Moose once more. "Is there anything you can do for a hundred?"

"Let's talk about this in the van," I said, pulling Moose away from Toucan.

When we got to the van, I let Toucan and Moose in on the passenger side first. Then I loaded Mrs. Hawkins onto the hydraulic chairlift. She was still motionless with her head drooped downward. The patch on her forehead was now dry and slightly scabbed over. I poked it with my forefinger to see just how healed it was. She didn't wince when I tapped the lesion on her head. Her eyes didn't even blink. That's when I became scared. Mrs. Hawkins was never very active, but she had her ways of expressing herself. She would do things like blink, raise and lower her eyebrows, slightly move her left hand, and undulate her jaw. To most people those movements were almost unnoticeable, but to someone who deeply cared for Mrs. Hawkins, like myself, they were as loud as a foghorn. It was a language that I was fluent in. That's why I knew she didn't have a problem with me watching her sponge baths. She would raise her eyebrows upward and open her eyes wider. I took that to mean she liked the attention. Reminiscing on those times, I now looked at her closely and didn't see her chest moving.

"You need some help, man?" Toucan asked from the front seat.

"No," I replied, "everything's cool. This chairlift can be a little temperamental at times." I fastened Mrs. Hawkins' seat belt across her, and as I did so, I felt for a pulse on the side of her neck, there was none. She was dead. I froze temporarily as panicked thoughts ran through my mind. I suddenly found myself in a deep hole. Mrs. Hawkins was dead.

"You sure you don't need any help? You're kind of taking a long time back there." His words sounded distant to my ears. Mrs. Hawkins was dead. I couldn't believe it. All that ran through my mind was Amanda. She was not going to like this. She was going to blame me, of course. I needed a way out.

"Hey, Toucan."

"Yeah?"

"You got time to go on a drive?" I asked.

"Why, what's up?" I closed Mrs. Hawkins' door and walked up the driver's seat.

"I'll tell you on the way."

SUNDAY 2:44 P.M.

We headed to McDonald forest and drove down a random trail until the van had difficulty moving forward. Deciding that to be the best parking place, I turned the van off and climbed out.

"So what exactly are we doing here?" Toucan asked, while walking Moose to my side of the van. I unfastened Mrs. Hawkins' seat belt and lowered the chairlift.

"You can let him run free out here," I said pointing to Moose. "He ain't gonna bother anyone out here." I rested Mrs. Hawkins chair on the rocky soil. Toucan freed Moose from his leash. I always liked taking Moose out in nature. He seemed comfortable and happy in the forest, and seeing him happy and comfortable, made me happy and comfortable. True, today was an unhappy visit to the forest, but Moose did make me smile, albeit briefly.

"Hellllooooo?" I looked at Toucan with slanted eyebrows.

"What?"

"Why'd you drive me to the middle of nowhere just to sell me a bag of weed?"

"Why? Opportunity, Toucan, that's why." I started pushing Mrs. Hawkins up the steep hill. Toucan followed behind at a safe distance. Moose occasionally crossed our path, further ahead, following various scents and rodents. He loved the outdoors.

"Look, I can just wait in the car while you and the old lady go for a hike." I stopped and looked back at him.

"True, you could. Maybe I could leave you with your $100 worth of weed too?" Toucan's face suddenly brightened as he roared in approval.

"That's what I'm talking about," he said while slapping his hands together.

"Or..." I said slowly in a high tone aimed at being intriguing, "you could hike with us and get an ounce for your measly hundred bucks." Toucan looked at me and laughed softly to himself.

"Measly? You didn't even know how much an ounce was worth until I told you at the skate..."

"Look," I interrupted, "do you want an ounce for a hundred bucks or not?"

"Well, yeah, but I don't want to do anything that'll..."

"Did I say you had to do anything?" He stood quiet with a confused expression on his face. He looked like he was trying to figure something out. I had decided to interrupt him whenever I felt he was getting close to making sense. This went on for a couple of minutes and proved much harder than I thought it would be. How could a man insane enough to believe you could eat sunlight, be smart enough to know I was trying to pin a murder on him? He was a walking paradox. "Look, let's just go for a friendly walk up this hill.

Then we'll come back, and I'll sell you the weed. Can you do that for me?" He nodded silently and followed me up the hill.

Pushing a wheelchair up a rocky hill is neither easy nor pleasurable. A heavy sweat was starting to gather on my forehead and in my armpits. I thought about asking Toucan to help me but decided against it. It was hard enough to get him to accompany me willingly up the hill, no sense in asking anything more of him. After what felt like thirty minutes, but was probably closer to ten, we reached a small plateau and rested. Moose was foaming at the mouth with thirst. The plateau was only about 30 square feet with forest flanking one side, and a cliff on the other. The drop off had to be close to 50 feet. At the bottom of the cliff there was a narrow stream carving its way through tall pine trees and jagged, gray rocks into a small lake.

"How much longer are we gonna walk?" asked Toucan. I kicked a rock over the edge and watched it fall to the ground.

"Why, you got somewhere to be?" I asked sarcastically. He looked at me with an expression that hinted at both embarrassment and anger. He knew he had nowhere to be, and no one waiting on him. A deep sigh was his gesture of agreeing to be patient and wait quietly for his ounce. For some reason I felt bad for embarrassing him. In a polite tone I asked, "You wanna give me a hand with something?"

"I thought you said I didn't have to do anything."

"Well, Toucan, I… I guess I lied. But, if it makes you feel better, I promise I'll sell you the ounce after you help me with this one little favor." He sighed again and walked toward me.

"What do you want me to do?"

"It's simple," I said, "all I need you to do is help me toss Mrs. Hawkins over the cliff, into that lake down there." I pointed over the cliff to the lake. Toucan's eyes opened wide and his mouth dropped.

"What? No way, man! I'm not going to help you kill an old lady!"

"Toucan, calm down. If it makes you feel any better, she's already dead." He was visibly nervous. He rubbed his hands together and looked side to side, as if peering for a hidden camera.

"I can't do that, man, I don't need weed that bad!" He held his hands up by his shoulders and opened his eyes wide. "Why do you want to kill her anyway?"

"I told you, she's already dead. I just need to get rid of her body." He looked at me with a stupefied expression. As he opened his mouth to comment, I continued. "Okay listen, she asked me to do this for her. She didn't want the big funeral and grave underground. She wanted to return to nature as quickly as possible. You just had to know Mrs. Hawkins the way I did. She was a free spirit. She thought outside the box. This is a prime example of it." He didn't look any more convinced. "Trust me, I'm not getting you in any trouble." This was all a lie of course, but the interesting aspect, to me at least, was how effortlessly these lies came to me. It was like I had a natural talent for deceiving people.

"So, she *wanted* this?" Toucan asked hesitantly.

"Yes, Toucan, these were her wishes." I almost smiled at the quality of lie I had constructed on the spot. I was kind of impressed with myself. But then a glance at Toucan in his black trench coat, acid washed jeans, and purple shirt reminded me that I wasn't exactly fooling a genius here.

"We just toss her in the lake down there and leave? No one asks any questions?"

I was becoming tired of his apprehension. "Jesus Christ, Toucan! Let's just toss her off the cliff and get high. I'll deal with the red tape. No one will ever know you were here, I promise." He stood motionless for what felt like an eternity before silently nodding in agreement.

I lifted her out of the wheelchair, laid her body on the ground, and started undressing her.

"Why are you undressing her?" asked Toucan.

"Because we can't leave any evidence lying around, duh! If she's nude she'll decompose faster, or animals can eat her more easily. It's kind of obvious isn't it, Toucan?"

"I don't think…"

"You don't need to think, Toucan! All you need to do is what I ask of you, okay?" He mumbled something, then shrugged and shook his head.

Removing Mrs. Hawkins' clothes again struck me with her beauty. Even at 83 years-old she still had curves. Most elderly women had saggy bags of flesh for breasts, but not Mrs. Hawkins. Her breasts were still full and semi-round. She had soft freckles around her nipples. I caressed the surprisingly tight skin near her areola.

"Dude, did you just rub her boob?"

"What? No, I didn't! I didn't just...I thought there was a fly on it."

"You thought there was a fly on her boob?"

"Yes, Toucan, I thought there was a fly on her boob. Is that so hard to believe?"

"But she's dead. Why would it matter if there was a fly..."

"Will you just shut up? Stop talking! I know what I'm doing. Take her pants off and help me pick her up." We put her clothes in the now discarded wheelchair.

It was time to throw her into the lake. I held her under her shoulders, while Toucan held her legs. We separated until her wrists were in my hands and her ankles in Toucan's. Our eyes locked and I whispered, "On three." We slowly swung her limp body back and forth, gently. As the momentum built to a climax, I counted, "One, two, three!" And on three we heaved Mrs. Hawkins' corpse over the cliff.

At first, I thought we put too much muscle into our throw, because she looked to be sailing over the small lake, however, gravity soon took control of her descent and it appeared she would fall short of the target. She slowly plummeted and turned counterclockwise in midair. My fear of her falling onto the lake's shore was assuaged when her body barley cleared the last set of jagged rocks. She hit the water with a loud splash that echoed off the surroundings. Her body disappeared under the lake's surface before emerging a few seconds later.

"Shit!" I said in disgust, "I forgot dead bodies float."

SUNDAY 4:20 P.M.

The drive back to Lumpy's was a silent one. Besides the near constant raising and lowering of his window, Toucan hardly made a sound. Now that I had dealt with Mrs. Hawkins, I found my mind filled with possible setbacks. What if some father and son found her body on a weekend fishing trip? What was I going to do with her wheelchair? How was I going to explain her absence from Harrington's? These are the fears that ran through my head as I stared blankly at a red stoplight.

Toucan finally broke the silence. "So, that's some story we've got now."

I slowly turned my gaze from the stoplight to his face. "Yeah, tell me about it," I said, before shaking my head back and forth. The light turned green. "You want me to drop you off at Lumpy's?" I knew what the answer to this question would be, so I headed that direction before he had a chance to respond. We parked across the street from Lumpy's and unbuckled our seat belts.

"So, can I get that ounce for you now or what?" Toucan asked in a whisper.

"Oh yeah," I answered, "you got the hundred dollars?"

"You're really going to make me pay you? I was kind of hoping… after helping you with the old lady…that…"

"Toucan, if I just went around giving weed to every person who helped me discard of a body, I'd never make any money, now would I?" He gave me a horrified expression.

"Perhaps it's too early to joke about it," I said in a hushed tone, "but seriously, I'm gonna need that hundred dollars." He handed me the money, and I handed him the weed.

"Why's it in a sock?"

"It's a long story, but it's all there. Now listen, Toucan, when you go inside Lumpy's you can't say anything about what we did today. It has to be our secret…forever!"

Toucan stopped smelling the sock and looked at me. "I don't think that'll be a problem. It's not like I'm going to tell people I helped kill an old lady. It's not the type of thing that just pops up in a conversation."

He stepped out of the van and closed the door behind him. I watched him cross the street and enter the bar. For some reason I felt Toucan to be the least of my worries. My real concern was back at Harrington's. How was I going to explain Mrs. Hawkins' absence to Amanda and the rest of the staff? I started the van back up and headed home. The day's events played in my mind over and over. I searched for a silver lining. On the upside, I had spent the majority of my shift driving Mrs. Hawkins around. True, my day had culminated with manslaughter and a body drop, but it still beat dispensing pills and cleaning old people all day.

Moose began to whimper when we reached the house. That was one of the only qualities I disliked about him. For being such a large and intimidating dog, I couldn't understand why he made such wimpy noises. I knew it came from excitement, such as seeing one of his favorite people, getting to go on a walk, or having to use the restroom; I just thought it should be a deeper, more macho sound. It should have matched his appearance. I parked the van in the driveway, put the sock of weed in the green backpack, and hopped out of the van.

When we entered the house, he ran straight for the back door. I let him out and watched him do his monotonous routine of sniff, spin, shit. He, no doubt, had been holding it in for quite a while.

While he finished up outside, I threw the backpack on the kitchen table and grabbed a drink from the fridge. In doing this, I noticed the phone's message light was blinking. I picked it up expecting to hear a message from Rachel, but it was Amanda's voice that greeted my ear. The message was over two hours old. I erased it before its conclusion. She said something about calling her back, it was important, or something like that. Whatever. She'd be getting her prize when I returned to Harrington's. Once I showed up without Mrs. Hawkins, Amanda would be calling the police to come get me, and I'd be getting booked with murder or at least manslaughter. I let Moose back inside and rolled another joint. If I was going to walk into a shitty situation, I was going to do so high as hell! No sense in facing incarceration sober. I lit the joint, sat on the couch with Moose, and watched some show with a judge berating white trash litigants for making poor life decisions. It might have been a rerun. I felt at peace.

SUNDAY 5:15 P.M.

After eating a quart of mint chocolate chip ice cream, I took the sock of weed from the backpack and stuffed it into a cereal box on top of my fridge- figured it was a good hiding spot. It was time to return to Harrington's and accept my fate. There was no way I was going to evade the punishment I deserved; Amanda would make sure of that. I parked the van in its designated spot, left Mrs. Hawkins' wheelchair and clothes inside, and closed the door behind me. Before I locked it, I remembered the yellow service note it had had on the gear shift when I entered. I put it back in place and closed the door once more. I tried to walk as slowly as possible. My hope was to take in every aspect of the day, seeing as it might be the last free one of my life. The wind was gentle and blew from east to west. The sky was slowly turning from blue to amber with streaks of golden light reaching like fingers across the postcard image. I inhaled heavily and closed my eyes. It's funny how we often need something terrible like Mrs. Hawkins' death to make us slow down and appreciate the things we have. I was so set on getting Rachel back that I failed to realize how much happier I would be without her. The one pity lay a month would be missed, but she had a right to find what she valued. We all have that right. I was too caught up in the machismo of me versus Sean. The old, "He can't take my woman without a fight!" nonsense. I was an idiot. Through this whole ordeal I again came to realize that the only companion I truly needed in my life was Moose. That's why dogs are called man's best friend. They give us everything we need in life, except sex of course.

I walked in the back door since it was the closest to the van parking lot. In the men's locker room I found Ruben reading the paper on a bench by the lockers. He hardly paid me any attention.

"You finally back?" he asked without looking up from his paper.

"Yeah, I...I just went for a drive. What are you doing here so early?" He folded his paper and looked up at me.

"They called me in early. Amanda said you took the van in to get serviced. They didn't know when you were coming back."

I stopped in my tracks. "Amanda said that?"

"Yeah. She said she called you and everything, but you didn't call back." He continued talking, but I stopped listening.

"Ruben," I interrupted, "I'm not trying to be rude, but I need to get upstairs. You look good though. You losing weight?" I left the locker room while Ruben responded with an indecipherable comment. Ruben was a good man, but he was boring. He was often the mental picture that came to mind when I imagined what it would be like to never do anything wrong. I would ask myself, "Don't you know better than this?" And I would always respond, "Yes, but if I always do what's right, I'd essentially become Ruben." Then in a condescending mental voice I'd ask myself, "Is that what you want? Do you want to be just like Ruben?" At which point my ego would loudly protest, and stupidly lead me into some mischievous behavior...such as taking a crippled Mrs. Hawkins out of Harrington's. It's amazing how little we men mature after the age of 17.

I jumped in the elevator and rode it to the dreaded third floor. Why would Amanda say I took the van to get serviced? She had unknowingly provided me with an alibi for taking the van out. Now I could use her reasoning against her in an argument. If she blamed me for Mrs. Hawkins missing, I would use the Good Samaritan excuse against her. "Why are you yelling at me? I was only taking the van to get its brakes, or engine, or whatever fixed. I wish I could tell you where your Aunt was, but I have no idea. I'm sorry." She had already won the argument for me. My alibi was so good that she not only believed it herself, she concocted it as well. The elevator doors dinged and I walked into the third-floor lobby. Amanda was behind the desk, on a telephone, having what appeared to be a very animated conversation. When she saw me, her eyes opened wide and she motioned me in her direction. I was prepared for her this time.

"What's up Manders? Looks like you're caught up in an important conversation. I'll catch up with you later." I casually walked away with one hand in my pocket, while waving to others with my free hand. I thought it looked presidential.

"Wait!" she screamed from behind me.

I turned around and looked at her with my best "I didn't just kill your great aunt facial" expression. "What's up, Mandy? You need something?" I tried to say this in an understanding voice, but it came off extremely condescending. I almost cringed at the sound of it.

"Yeah, I do need something. And don't call me Mandy. What am I twelve?"

"Sorry," I said while shrugging my shoulders, "I didn't know abbreviating your name was such a sore spot, but I'm glad I've learned something about you. Listen, I'm gonna go take care of a few things. We'll talk later." I tried to walk past her, but she grabbed my shoulder sleeve and pulled me toward her.

"No, you listen!" she said as forcefully as her hippie demeanor would allow. "First off, I let you call me Manders, so don't push it! I could report your little nickname name for me to management as sexual harassment, but I've let it slide!"

"I don't see how Manders could be taken as a sexual…"

"And second of all," she continued with the same fervor, "you still haven't told me where Mrs. Hawkins is!" She paused for a couple seconds as if waiting for me to divulge Mrs. Hawkins' secret whereabouts. After an awkward amount of silence had passed, she continued with her spiel. "I covered for your ass! I told them you took the van to get serviced."

She paused again. I think she was still hoping my conscience would speak up. She didn't know that that little voice in my head, the one that tells you when to do the right thing, had all but died long ago. How else could I possibly be able to look her in the eye after tossing her great aunt off of a cliff? Maybe the weed helped me a little, but mostly it was because my conscience was on life support.

"Amanda, I don't know where she is. I told you that last time you asked me."

"That was over six hours ago! How do you expect me to believe a partially paralyzed, 85-year-old woman just got up and walked out of here?" She exhaled a deep breath and pushed some of her red hair behind her left ear.

"I saw her in the van with you," she continued. "Please, I just want to find my grandmother," she put her hands over her face and started a soft sob.

Shocked, and now overwhelmingly confident, I stood across from her. It appeared to me that Amanda had gone to the sympathy well one too many times and gotten lost. For starters, Mrs. Hawkins was 83 years-old, not 85. And secondly, Amanda had said Mrs. Hawkins was her great aunt earlier, not her grandmother. How does one forget a family member's title so quickly? It seemed fishy to me.

"I thought you said Mrs. Hawkins was your great aunt?"

Amanda froze and fumbled for an answer. Before she could put together a coherent answer, I continued. "And I believe Mrs. Hawkins is 83 years old, not 85. What's up with your misinformation? You must not be as close as you're trying to portray." I stood silent and waited for Amanda to explain herself.

"Follow me." she said and turned toward an empty room. Her auburn hair bounced as she walked quickly away from me. I followed behind her, unsure of what I was about to be told. We went inside the room and she closed the door behind me.

"So what's so important we had to come in here?" I asked as she walked away from the door.

Amanda strolled over to the window and looked at the view before responding. When she finally did turn around, her facial expression was one I had never seen on her before. She looked defeated. I was accustomed to seeing Amanda smug and giggly, but now she appeared deflated.

"I was talking to Martha on the phone when you came in" she began, "we were talking about your trip. I told Martha not to come in today, because I wanted to teach you a lesson."

I looked at Amanda in amazement. Who did she think she was? Who was she to teach me a lesson? Before I could scream at her, she started talking again.

"It just made me sick, the way you're always looking at Mrs. Hawkins. It's like you're actually attracted to her. So when I heard about you and Martha's trip with the patients, I took it upon myself to destroy it."

"So you're the reason Mr. Rash and the others decided not to come?" I asked.

"Yeah…kind of."

"What do you mean kind of?"

"Well I did talk the others out of going, but not Mr. Rash. He said he wanted to tell you to your face that he wasn't going. He called you a natural born loser or something like that."

"Damn Mr. Rash! I hate that guy!" I said to myself silently.

"But I couldn't keep you from Mrs. Hawkins," continued Amanda, "so I traded shifts with Martha and made up a story about her being my great aunt or grandmother. I was trying to appeal to your compassionate side." Her eyes started to water, but this time it was real. "Now I can't find Mrs. Hawkins and it's all my fault. That's why I said you took the van to get serviced. I hoped that if I helped you, you'd help me."

She again stopped talking and gazed out the window. I looked her up and down trying to gauge her sincerity. She held her arms folded in front of her and softly swayed side to side while her eyes watered. There were three painted wood beads in her hair that gave her a bohemian look. Even though she appeared to be earthy, Amanda was quite uptight at times. This appeared to be one of those times. I started to feel bad for her and wanted to help her out, until I remembered Mrs. Hawkins' lifeless body was floating in a shallow lake in McDonald forest. That kind of put the gravity of the situation into perspective.

"So you're not related to Mrs. Hawkins?" I asked calmly.

"No." she replied without looking at me.

I studied her closely before asking my next question. "Does anyone else know she's missing?"

She wiped a tear and cleared her throat before responding. "Not yet. I've been making up excuse after excuse to keep people out of her room, but I don't know how much longer that's going to work. They're going to notice she's gone sooner or later."

I waited for what felt like an hour before finally answering her plea for help. Here were the facts: Amanda had been a bitch lately...that was a bad thing. However, she was not related to Mrs. Hawkins...that was a good thing. Mrs. Hawkins was dead...that was a very bad thing. Amanda had beads in her hair...that didn't mean much by itself, but it helped paint a bigger picture. She also attended the local college. Again, by itself, not an important fact, but it added to the picture. Lastly, she was deathly afraid of getting in trouble for losing Mrs. Hawkins. Combined, these facts painted a young, bohemian, potential pot smoker stuck in a desperate situation. If I could offer her a way out of this mess, she might unwittingly help me avoid punishment as well. Impunity. Therefore, I decided the key to both of our troubles was the ounce of weed in my cereal box at home. It was times like these that made me think there just might be a God after all.

Gently, I place my hand on Amanda's shoulder. "Okay, you're right. I do know where Mrs. Hawkins is at." She breathed a small sigh of relief. "I'll help you out, but you've got to do something for me first."

She looked at me with red, watery eyes. "What is it?"

"I need you to find a way out of here for us. Once you've done that, meet me in the van outside."

SUNDAY 5:41 P.M.

I left Amanda and hurried back to the van. Everything was just how I'd left it, Mrs. Hawkins' clothes were still folded on the back seat, and her wheelchair was still sitting on the chairlift. I was suddenly glad I had forgotten to put the van key back when I returned to Harrington's. Every piece of evidence needed to convict me of Mrs. Hawkins' death was locked inside this van. After about ten minutes, Amanda finally showed up and climbed in the van. She looked behind her and saw Mrs. Hawkins' belongings.

"I told Ruben we were going to get a bite...Are those her clothes?" she asked in a frightened tone.

"We need to go on a drive," I said, fastening my seat belt. "You might want to buckle up for this one." I started the van and put it in reverse.

On the drive to Arby's, then to my house, I entertained Amanda with a tale about evil teenagers and the skate park. I told her it was there that these corrupt souls had taken Mrs. Hawkins from me, and now I had no idea where she was. While I was bringing my amazingly exaggerated tale to a conclusion, I manufactured a weak stream of tears by remembering my childhood dog, Buster, who died in a house fire. That story used to bring rivers of tears to my eyes when I was younger, but I guess time has a way of damming rivers of pain. I parked the van in my driveway and cut its engine off.

She sat silently and digested my story. I thought about turning the radio on to muffle the silence. "So, are you telling me Mrs. Hawkins is dead?" she finally asked.

"I'm not telling you she's dead, I'm telling you they, the skateboarders, took her from me and I don't know where she is." She stared out the passenger window before turning to ask another question.

"And how, exactly, did they take her from you?"

"I told you, I went to the bathroom, and when I came out, she was gone. All they left was Moose and her chair."

"And her clothes?"

"What?"

"Her clothes," Amanda repeated. "They left Moose, her chair, and her clothes behind."

I fumbled for a response. "Well, yeah...they left her clothes too."

"Exactly how long were you in the bathroom?"

I nervously chuckled at her question. "I can't tell you the exact amount of time I was in the bathroom, Amanda, but I can tell you it was a paper reader, if you know what I mean." She scrunched her face at my remark, apparently not impressed with my bathroom vernacular.

"I've gotta get Moose back inside. You wanna wait out here or come in for a minute?" She answered by opening her door and stepping out of the van. I hopped in the back and led Moose through the van's sliding door.

Once inside the house, I let Moose out the back door and assumed he would do his ritualistic sniff, spin, piss, and shit. He was the only person unchanged by the day's events.

"You got anything to drink?" she asked. I poured her a glass of orange juice from the fridge.

"Do you think we should call Ruben and check in with him?" I asked while bringing her drink to her. She shook her head side to side before swallowing a few gulps.

"No," she said, putting her glass down, "Ruben owes me a favor or two. I covered nearly an entire shift for him last week. He had a dentist appointment, but management wouldn't let him have the day off on such short notice, so I told him he owed me one." She leaned back on the couch and seemed to relax a bit.

I looked at her closely and pondered the relationship that her and Ruben had, and why it had never been apparent to me.

"Besides," she continued, "we can't go back until you find Mrs. Hawkins."

Hearing Mrs. Hawkins' name snapped me out of my daydream with a flinch I was sure Amanda noticed. I tried to play it off by walking to the door to let Moose back inside. He was ready to come in and take a nap. This had been a long day for him. However, finding

Amanda in his favorite napping location, he was forced to lie on a small rug in the corner of the living room.

Amanda had started to talk again, but I wasn't paying her much attention. I had looked at the clock and noticed it was almost 6 o'clock. I was supposed to meet that guy from Walmart at Lumpy's any minute now. That wasn't going to happen now. I had more important things to do, like hopefully getting Amanda high enough to believe a bunch of skaters had stolen Mrs. Hawkins.

"Are you listening to anything I'm saying?"

I looked at her and instantly started nodding my head. "Of course I was listening to you." I paused and took a deep breath. "It's just…I'm thinking about Mrs. Hawkins. We need to find her."

Slightly annoyed, Amanda slowly shook her head side to side. A wisp of auburn hair fell in front of her face and she tucked it behind her ear. "Obviously you weren't listening, because that's exactly what I was talking about!" She started shaking her head again. "You can be such an asshole, you know that?"

I didn't answer her question; I don't think she really wanted one. It always bothered me when people asked questions they didn't want answers to. And women did it all the time. That was part of the reason a Vietnamese wife appealed to me in the first place. I hadn't bargained on Rachel being such a quick study. In a mere two years she had become the prototypical American woman. I thought back to her breakup speech.

Again, Amanda broke my daydream, this time by screaming, "Hello! You don't have anything to say to that?"

"Yes, Amanda, I do have something to say to that. First of all, there's no need for name calling. Second of all, I think we're both a little stressed out and need to collect our composure." I waited for a response, but all she did was sit quietly and fold her arms.

"Now stop me if I offend you Amanda, but I see the wood beads in your hair, and I think I know what helps you relax." I walked over to the fridge and grabbed the cereal box on top of it.

"You think Lucky Charms is going to help me regain my composure?" she asked in a sarcastic tone.

"No," I said, ignoring her tone, "I think it's what's inside the box that will help us calm down." I pulled out the near ounce of weed and her eyes went wide.

"*You* smoke weed?" she asked in amazement.

"Don't you?" I responded.

"Why, because I have a few wood beads in my hair?"

"And you're a college kid." I added.

"Oh, so every college aged kid with beads in their hair smokes weed?" She looked at me as if hurt by the accusation.

I waited a few seconds before responding with what seemed like the most logical observation. "You still haven't said you don't smoke, Amanda."

SUNDAY 6:14 P.M.

As Amanda and I passed a can of Pringles back and forth, our conversation did what many stoned conversations did; drifted from one topic to another. We talked about pollution, politics, and work. Like most twenty-one-year-olds, she had no clue what she was talking about, but her ignorance was kind of cute. She was also a surprisingly good listener. I actually enjoyed getting high with her. Her constant giggling and naïve perception of the world made me smile. However, my smile was erased when she started asking about my wife.

"How long have you two been separated?" she asked with genuine concern.

"A couple months," I lied. I didn't want to say we had officially separated only a few days ago. It made me sound a little skuzzy. Plus, it wasn't entirely accurate. After all, Rachel had openly been dating Sean for almost a year. I just wanted to sound confused and slightly vulnerable. Women found that attractive in men for some reason. And I, for reasons beyond my grasp, was trying to appeal to Amanda.

"We should get out of here," I said, and placed my hand gently on her thigh.

"Yeah, you're probably right." She put her hand on mine. "Thanks for smoking with me. I've always said it's the *second-*

best way to relieve stress." She looked in my eyes and flashed a coy smile.

I leaned closer, pressed my lips against her neck, and whispered in her ear, "Well what's the best way to relieve stress, Amanda?" Before she could answer, I grabbed a handful of her breast and kissed her earlobe.

"Are you sure you're ready to be intimate with someone so soon?" she asked in between kisses to my mouth and neck.

I shoved my tongue down her throat and wrapped my fingers in her hair. "I'm a man, Amanda." She looked into my eyes waiting for further explanation. "The best way for a man to get over someone, is on top of someone else." And with that I kissed her again. We groped each other as we stood up and fumbled down the hall. When we made it to my room, I turned the lights on and laid her on top of the bed. After a couple minutes of making out and undressing, she asked me to wait a second.

"What's the matter?" I asked, obviously annoyed.

"Don't you have any blinds or curtains? Your neighbors can see right in here."

I stood up and slowly undressed. "If they wanna watch…let 'em. Maybe they'll learn a thing or two." Not only did I say this cheesy line in my sexiest voice possible, I also posed nude to enhance its sentiment. She must have agreed, or at least thought me funny because she giggled and said nothing more about it.

I kissed her neck and removed her shirt. She had small, perky, slightly odd-shaped breasts, with very nice nipples. I liked them. Most women don't know this, but a good-looking set of nipples can salvage an otherwise ugly pair of breasts. This was true in Amanda's case. She was definitely telling the truth about *not* being related to Mrs. Hawkins.

After she was undressed, I stood up and looked at her naked body. She had a slim figure with faint freckles all over. It was the kind of body you would expect on a young earthy chick; skinny, but curvy. Womanly, but petite. I was amazed I had never noticed her sex appeal before. But then again, I had never seen her in anything but her Harrington's uniform, and it's hard to look sexy in smocks.

What ensued after the removal of Amanda's clothes was seven to ten minutes of surprisingly good sex. This was perfect for me. That's all I was good for. I've never been a fan of marathon intercourse. Who can't make a woman orgasm in an hour's time? Try doing it in a matter of minutes; that takes skill. I always viewed sex as a race, or friendly competition. Whoever climaxes first wins. I seldom lost. Perhaps I was too competitive in that regard.

When we finished, I rolled over and played with her hair for a little while. "You wanna smoke again?" I asked.

SUNDAY 6:58 P.M.

Remembering the plan, I grabbed the green backpack from off the kitchen table and led Amanda out of the house. She petted Moose on the head before closing the front door behind her. I asked if she was sure she had locked it. She made a snide remark under her breath and got in the van. There was an awkward tension between us as we drove away from my house. Why does that happen? What is it about sex that makes human beings so uneasy? I mean if you're willing to do something that personal with someone, shouldn't it bring you closer together? Made sense to me. But when I looked at Amanda, I didn't see someone who felt closer to me. I saw a young girl who appeared to be regretting having slept with me. I almost laughed. It was starting to feel that no matter who the woman, whether born in the United States, or purchased overseas, they simply didn't enjoy my style of lovemaking. I shrugged my shoulders at the notion. Perhaps I was ahead of my time in the bedroom. Perhaps women weren't ready for my fast-paced passion. I laughed under my breath and decided it was their problem, not mine. A leopard can't change its spots, and a man can't change his style of lovemaking. It's just unnatural.

We headed back to Harrington's slowly. I wanted to check out Lumpy's first. The Walmart guy was on my mind. Had he showed up like he said he would? If so, did he think I was a flake?

I certainly hoped not. I'm not quite sure why, but I've always hated being viewed as a flake. If I give my word on something, I do all I can to keep it. I felt you had to, otherwise your word doesn't mean anything. Therefore, I needed to at least check if he had shown up. That way if I ever saw him again, I could say, "Hey, what happened to you the other day? I was there, where were you?" I needed that higher ground.

We drove about five blocks before Amanda started to question my route. "Where are we going?" she asked in a rather uppity tone. I wondered what happened to the sweet, innocent girl on my couch.

"Relax," I said, "we're going back to Harrington's. I've just got a few stops to make." She looked at me with a less than flattering expression. Why was she so irritated?

"Hey, Amanda."

"What?"

"I want you to know I really enjoyed what happened back at my house. I mean, I never knew you looked at me that way. To be honest, I always thought you kind of…"

"Oh, Jesus! Really?"

I stopped talking and looked at her. "Really… what?" I asked in a soft voice.

"Are you *really* going to get all touchy feely with me now?" She waited for a response. I had none. "Look, you got me high. I get a little horny when I'm high. It just happened. No need to go and make more out of it than what it was, okay?" She paused again. I still had no reply. "So do me a favor and spare me your emotions about how the sex changed your opinion of me, cured cancer, or helped feed some starving child in Africa somewhere. It was just sex!"

She went on to mumble something about men not being able to separate emotions from sex. I didn't listen too closely. I didn't need to- she was right. Men see women as beautiful expanses of land or territory. Once a man sleeps with a woman, he feels he can return at any time to roam that plot of land again. Like a lion, we feel it's our domain. Now while those may not be the exact emotions Amanda was speaking of, they are emotions all the same, therefore, whether she knew it or not, she was right in what she said. We drove to Lumpy's without saying another word to each other.

When we pulled into Lumpy's parking lot, I told Amanda I'd only be inside a second. She made no indication of having heard me and continued to look out the window. I couldn't get out of that van fast enough. I left the engine running and ran inside the bar. Garret was still bartending. Remembering our last conversation, I thought it wise to move in and out as fast as possible. Garret was a dumb ass, no reason to make an interaction with him longer than it needed to be.

"Hey, asshole!" I heard, shouted in my direction as I scanned the back-wall for the Walmart guy. "Hey, asshole, I'm talking to you!" I turned slowly and faced the bar.

"What do you want, Garret?" He finished wiping a glass and threw a bar towel over his shoulder like some bartender in an old sepia tone motion picture. He was such a tool.

"I thought I told you not to come in here again." He was clearly getting off on this attempted power-trip. He readjusted the towel on his shoulder before continuing. "Maybe you don't hear so good? You need me to say it in Espanol? El-you-o are-o el-not-o welcome here, el-asshole-o." He laughed with the drunks in front of him who apparently found his lame attempt at Spanish humorous. I wondered why "welcome here" didn't have any el or o's attached to it. Finding no other reason than him being an idiot, I decided it was time to defend myself.

"First of all, Garrett, I'm not Hispanic. And second of all, that was the worst Spanish imitation I've ever heard. I've heard Japanese men with better Spanish accents than that." I moved my focus from him and looked for the Walmart guy. He didn't appear to be anywhere in sight. I was about to leave when Garrett stepped out from behind the bar.

"Now you listen here," he said, in the best "badass" voice he could muster. "I don't care if you're Mexican, Spanish, or goddamn Latino, (he said every culture with air quotes); "I don't like you. I don't like you in my bar, and I sure as hell don't like you bringing dirty dogs and old ladies in here. You're suspended for a week." He opened his eyes wide and slowly nodded his head up and down.

He felt important. It didn't matter to him that his punishment was toothless.

I responded without looking at him. "See you tomorrow, Garrett." I turned around and found him standing directly in my path. Amanda was still in the van, and she was probably wondering what was taking me so long. I started for the door and shoulder bumped Garrett on my way past. He was definitely in better shape than I was, but he was smaller and skinnier than I was. He stumbled a few steps backwards after our collision. Then he yelled something again about kicking my ass next time he saw me. I was actually glad the Walmart guy hadn't shown up; I couldn't stand much more time inside that bar. Why do some people never mature past their junior year of high school?

Amanda was still sitting in the passenger seat with a bored expression on her face. I wondered what she could be thinking. The van door squeaked as I climbed back in and buckled my seat belt.

"Did you find whoever you were looking for?" she asked with mild interest.

"Actually, I did. And they told me the people we're looking for are down at the skatepark." I started the van and headed out of the parking lot.

"So… who are we looking for?" Amanda asked in the same mildly interested voice.

"We're looking for the bastards who stole Mrs. Hawkins, that's who we're looking for!" I pounded my fist on the dashboard for emphasis. I wanted her to know I was definitely not responsible for Mrs. Hawkins disappearance. Even though that was a blatant lie, I figured like most things in life, if you say it enough, you start to believe it's true. It's hard to call someone a liar when they actually believe what they're telling you. Women had mastered this philosophy over centuries. I was trying to learn on the fly.

Amanda scrunched her face numerous times before responding. "So let's recap here, shall we? You're telling me that you took Mrs. Hawkins to the skatepark. And while at the skatepark, you went to the restroom. And it was during this bathroom break that Mrs. Hawkins was lifted from her wheelchair, stripped nude, and stolen." She paused as if waiting for me to argue with something she had said. "Is this close to accurate? She asked.

"It's not just close to accurate, Amanda, it's like you were there!"

SUNDAY 7:34 P.M.

When we reached the skate park, we had been gone from Harrington's for almost two hours. Amanda was starting to worry about how we'd explain our absence when we eventually returned. The only reason she had even agreed to come to the skate park was the hope of finding Mrs. Hawkins. She felt that if we could find her, it would justify our extended absence from work. When I heard her say what she hoped we'd find at the park, I couldn't help but smile. I smiled because I, too, was hoping we'd find something at the park. I hoped to find the skaters who helped me get Mrs. Hawkins high, and then frame them for her death. That's why I smiled. And to be honest, I also smiled because, seeing as Mrs. Hawkins' body was dumped in a secluded lake, my hope was a lot more likely to be realized than was Amanda's. I paused briefly and wondered if Mrs. Hawkins' body was still floating? Surely, she had swallowed enough water by now to drown, but could dead people really swallow water? Either way, it couldn't have taken much, she barely weighed ninety pounds.

Before leaving the van, I grabbed Mrs. Hawkins' wheelchair and the green backpack. I opened the backpack and stuffed Mrs. Hawkins' clothes inside it. Everything I needed to frame the skater kids was now being pushed toward them on a cement park pathway. All I had to figure out was how I was going to give them the evidence, without tipping them off to the set up. Amanda was not making this any easier.

"Why are you taking the wheelchair to look for these guys?" she asked.

"Be-CAUSE, Amanda, I don't want them to suspect anything. Last time they saw me, I was pushing a wheelchair, it's called continuity." I sighed loudly and walked a few paces ahead of her.

Most of the park was empty, but that's what you had to love about skaters; they didn't have anywhere else to be. There were around fifteen kids in the skateboarder's section of the park. On first glance, I didn't see the kids I stole the weed from. However, on a second inspection, I saw two familiar faces; the skinny blonde kid who was more or less the ringleader, and the mannish, blonde girl with bad posture and a muscular build. I still thought he could do a lot better than her. We spotted each other at the same time. They made their way toward me, and I looked for a secluded place to lead them. The small patch of grass behind the bathrooms looked like the best spot to pull whatever it was I was trying to pull off. The blonde boy followed quickly, while the mannish girl lagged a good distance behind. As I pushed the wheelchair, it became quite clear to me that I hadn't thought this through very well. I knew I wanted to get their fingerprints on Mrs. Hawkins' wheelchair, but just how I was going to do that?

I hurried the wheelchair and backpack toward the restrooms. I glanced back over my shoulder and saw Amanda slowing down. She appeared to be watching the two skaters follow me. A sense of relief started to come over me. Amanda was there witnessing everything. That meant she could testify to my version of events if I ever needed her to. Hopefully it wouldn't come to that. Looking over my other shoulder, I noticed the skaters had slowed down as well.

They were looking at Amanda with puzzled expressions. Then the unthinkable happened.

"Drew?" Amanda said looking at the blonde boy.

"Amanda...what's up?" He looked from her to me. "You with this guy?" he asked while pointing a thumb at me.

"We're not together officially," I interrupted before she could respond, "but I think it's a definite possibility we could be, wouldn't you say so, Amanda?"

Her face winced as she replied, "No, I wouldn't say that. I wouldn't say that at all. He's a co-worker. We're looking...for...Sarah?" She was fixated on the mannish, blonde girl approaching.

"We're looking for who?" I asked softly. She either ignored my question or missed it entirely.

"What are you doing here, Sarah?" she continued. "Is *this* who you were talking about...*Drew?*"

I was thoroughly confused at what I was witnessing. I think Drew was too. We even exchanged bewildered glances at one another before turning our attention back to the girls. The blonde girl took a deep breath and exhaled slowly before speaking. "What does it matter, Amanda? It doesn't change anything between us anyway."

Amanda was visibly upset. "What does it matter?" she mimicked. "What does it matter, Sarah? Well, how 'bout for starters, it proves you're a whore?" Amanda folded her arms in front of her and smirked at the blonde girl. What ensued after that was a good five minutes of fast, high-pitched arguing. Seizing the opportunity, I looked at Drew and nodded. He tore his attention from the girls and turned toward me. I grabbed the backpack from the chair and shoved the wheelchair toward him.

"Push this and follow me," I said to him in a hushed voice. He placed his hands on Mrs. Hawkins' wheelchair and followed me behind the restrooms.

Watching him push Mrs. Hawkins' wheelchair, I studied Drew closely. He looked to be anywhere from 18 to 22 years old. He was about my height but couldn't have weighed more than a hundred and fifty pounds. He had a pierced lip and a pierced eyebrow. Though he tried to come off as tough, he had soft eyes. Eyes that showed kindness and vulnerability- and that, at times, can be a bad combination. He moved the wheelchair aside and approached me.

"You got my weed or what, bro?" he asked flatly. I rolled my eyes at his "bro" statement- so corny.

"Yeah, I've got your stuff," I said, patting the green backpack. "But..."

"But, what?" he asked.

I was stalling. "I don't think we should do the exchange here," I mumbled.

"What?"

I gave him a stern glance and slowly shook my head side to side. "We can't do it here," I said.

"Oh yeah, why?" He was obviously annoyed. I needed to come up with something quick.

"Because we're being watched," I blurted. "Did you ever think of that?" Drew's face went straight, and he looked at me with an expression of both caution and concern. It was obvious he wanted to hear more before he decided whether to panic or not.

"Who's watching us?" he asked curiously.

"Remember earlier today," I began, "when that cop walked me back to the van? Well, he asked if you were bothering us, me and Mrs. Hawkins that is, and I told him you weren't, but he said to watch out for you guys. Said you're trouble."

Drew waved his hands in the air. "Wait a minute," he said. "That cop told you that we're trouble?"

"He sure did, Drew. He said you guys come down here and do your drugs, and yell, and drink, and…piss all over the place. Said you don't do nothing but bother the community." When I finished speaking, I glanced over each shoulder as if I feared someone was watching our conversation.

Drew chuckled to himself and flashed an irritated smile. "I peed in a trash can one time," he said. "Damn cop acted like I shot somebody." He laughed and shook his head. "What a dick."

My eyes nearly popped out of my face, and I looked at the floor. "How lucky was that?" I asked myself. But then I answered my own question. Drew *did* strike me as the type of person that would urinate in a trash can. He was a punk. So maybe I wasn't lucky. Maybe I was smart. Either way, it didn't matter. I had to go with it now.

"Yeah, well, Drew, apparently it pissed him off." I paused, "No pun intended."

He chuckled once more and shook his head. "So where do you want to do the exchange?" he asked.

My mind raced for an answer. I began to fear I was taking too long to respond. The pace of the lies was catching up to me. "McDonald Forest," I finally managed to spit out. "There won't be anyone around up there," I said. "Let's meet up there in thirty minutes."

"McDonald Forest?" He seemed to be unhappy with my request. "Any specific location in McDonald Forest?" he asked. "It's a fucking national park, you know? Kind of a big place."

I looked at him in awe. Just when I was starting to second guess my actions, he goes along and acts like a smartass. Made my decision a lot easier, just like the entitled prick in high school, he needed to be taught a lesson. "Yeah, Drew, I've got a spot in mind." I rattled off directions to the lake behind a fake smile. I didn't want him to suspect anything, that's why I smiled. A kind face is always the best disguise for cruel intentions. Mandy Pickens taught me that lesson in twelfth grade. Rachel was teaching me that lesson now. Ironically, they both did it by sleeping with someone else. I found that coincidence odd.

I returned my focus to Drew. "So I'll see up there in a half hour?" I asked.

Drew shook his head. "I can't get up there," he said, "I ain't got no car, bro." Amanda and Sarah's argument seemed to be getting more intense.

"You haven't got a car?" I asked in shock. "What do you do, ride your skateboard everywhere, like a twelve-year-old?"

He looked at me as if I were stupid. "Yeah," he said, "that's what I do."

Somewhat embarrassed, and impatient, I looked Drew in the eyes. "Fine, Drew, how 'bout this? Take my work van and head up to the McDonald forest. You can drive, right?"

"Yeah, I can drive," he answered, almost offended. "But how are you and Amanda gonna get up there and meet us?"

"I live nearby," I lied, "I'll just run home and grab my car. I'll be there in thirty minutes, Drew. Don't leave me hanging." I was going to tell him not to steal the van, but I decided that wouldn't be such a bad thing, it would actually make it a whole lot easier to pin Mrs. Hawkins' death on him. I kind of hoped he'd steal it.

"So you're letting me take your work van to McDonald forest? And why do you trust me to show up?"

"Because I know you want your weed back." Knowing I was right, he stood and waited for me to speak again. "Okay. Here are the keys. The round one opens the back doors. You'll need to put the wheelchair back there."

"I'm taking the wheelchair too?" he complained.

"Drew, throw the wheelchair in the back of the van, and follow the directions I gave you to the lake. Can you do that?"

"Well yeah, but I don't think I..."

"I don't care what you think, Drew. That's the deal. Are you going to be there in thirty minutes or not?" I watched him fidget before agreeing. It's hard for men to be spoken to like that. We want to defend ourselves when attacked. This was true of Drew, except he knew I was right. He had no other way to the lake in McDonald forest, he wanted/needed his weed back, and he had to follow my guidelines if he wanted to get it. He was stuck.

"Fine," he muttered under his breath. "I'll be there in a half-hour." Then, as if to save face, he added, "Damn van better be an automatic!" I laughed and pushed Mrs. Hawkins wheelchair to him.

"Load this up," I said. "I'll send your girlfriend back to you." With that I turned and walked toward the screaming match that was Sarah and Amanda.

"It better be an automatic!" Drew repeated.

When I approached the two girls, Amanda was red in the face and crying. She was pointing at Sarah saying, "At least I know who I am!" Sarah, for her part, seemed entirely bored with the argument. She stood about four feet from Amanda with a disinterested expression. She rolled her eyes and played with her hair as Amanda spoke. It looked like a parent yelling at a teenager. I rushed to Amanda and put my hand on her shoulder.

"Everything okay?" I asked. They both looked at me in disbelief. "Sarah, is it?" I continued. "Drew said he needs you a minute, okay?" She looked from me to Amanda.

"Yeah, go ahead and walk away," Amanda snipped at her.

"Whatever," Sarah said while rolling her eyes once more. "You need to get a life," she said and turned toward Drew. Before Amanda could respond, I tossed her the green backpack and gently hurried her in the opposite direction.

"Come on," I said, pulling her along.

"I need to get a life?" she yelled. "I need to get a life? She doesn't even know who she is!"

"I know," I said, "let's just walk it off." As we strolled around the park, Amanda slowly calmed down. I asked her what all the fuss was over and she told me her and Sarah used to be lovers. I tried to tread lightly with my questions.

"So you're bisexual?" I asked. She sighed obviously annoyed with my question.

"Why are men like that?" she asked. Does everything have to be labeled? We just liked each other's company, that doesn't mean we're gay, or bi, or whatever."

"Well then...what would you call it?" I asked.

"Friends!" she responded.

"Friends who had sex?" I asked.

"Yes, friends who had sex, okay?"

I paused briefly before asking my next question. "Kind of like us?" I said softly. She stopped walking and looked sternly in my eyes.

"We're not friends," she said coldly, and began walking again.

After another minute or two of silence, Amanda seemed to be back to herself. She was still visibly angry, but nonetheless she apologized for the whole scene and gave me more details. It turns out she and Sarah had been "friends" for a couple of months. Then, without notice, Sarah started acting different. She didn't call as often, stayed out late, and seemed distant when she was around. I was amazed at how similar a lesbian relationship was to a heterosexual one. It sounded like we all cheated the same way. Betrayal knows no orientation. For some reason I thought of Rachel. Anyway, so after a month or so of this shady behavior, Amanda figured out what was going on, and her and Sarah stopped being "friends." She fell quiet and I figured the rest out on my own. Drew, obviously, was the person Sarah was cheating on Amanda with. That much I got. What I didn't get was why she was so upset by it? Weren't they just friends who had sex? If so, why would it matter if someone slept with someone else? Friends don't own each other. Or was it because Drew was a guy? And perhaps most confusing to me, why did they both find Sarah attractive? Was I the only one who thought she looked like a blonde primate?

SUNDAY 8:12 P.M.

After Amanda had finished her venting about Sarah, she sat on a picnic table and exhaled deeply. It was starting to get dark. Drew and Sarah had clumsily crammed Mrs. Hawkins' wheelchair into the van and left about ten minutes ago. Amanda had talked the entire time. I didn't mind her venting for two reasons, 1: it gave me sexy images to imagine, lesbian love, and 2: it distracted her from noticing Drew and Sarah had taken the van. Drew was expecting me to meet him in McDonald forest in twenty minutes. I had no intentions of making that appointment.

"What time is it?" Amanda asked from the picnic table.

"It's a quarter past eight," I answered. "You wanna get back? We've been gone a long time. Drew said he didn't have anything to do with Mrs. Hawkins disappearance, but what do you expect him to say?"

Amanda rose from the table and walked toward me. "Thanks for listening to me," she said. "That was nice of you." I smiled and told her it was no problem.

We headed back to the parking lot, and I prepared myself for the acting job of a lifetime. This was particularly stressful because

I was a terrible actor. I hadn't acted since *A Christmas Carol* in the seventh grade, and I was horrible then. My parents told me as much after the performance. They didn't do it to be rude; rather, they were just brutally honest. You had to respect them for that. What I didn't respect was my Dad's booing. Booing Tiny Tim? Too honest.

When we reached the parking lot, I put on my best bewildered face and scanned the parking lot from side to side. "Didn't we park here?" I asked in overemphasized tones. "I thought we…" I trailed off in hopes of appearing genuinely confused. I had a feeling I was bombing.

Amanda spun in a circle looking for the van. "Where's the van?" she asked. "Where's Mrs. Hawkins' wheelchair? What's going on?"

"I don't know," I replied. "You don't think Drew and Sarah had anything to do with this, do you?" The question was rhetorical. Amanda answered anyway.

"It's starting to look that way, isn't it?" she said.

"But Drew said he didn't have anything to do with Mrs. Hawkins' disappearance. Why would he steal the van and her wheelchair?" I pretended to be confused by Drew's apparent actions. I tried to imitate the kid in math class who does the algorithm mentally before saying the answer aloud. The finger movements, the soft mumbling, I did it all. After what felt like an hour, Amanda finally took the bait.

She placed her hands on her hips and looked me in the eyes. "I'll tell you why he did it," she said, "because he's lying, that's why."

"What do you mean?"

"Think about it," she said. "Why else would he steal the van and her wheelchair? He's trying to cover his tracks."

"Do you think Sarah would be a part of something like that?" I asked in curiosity.

Amanda paused before answering. She grabbed a wisp of her Auburn hair and wrapped it around her forefinger. "Before today," she began, "I would have said no way in hell, but obviously I don't know her as well as I thought I did." She cracked an unhappy smile and said, "Nothing would surprise me now."

Not wanting to waste any more time, I took my cell phone out and dialed 911. It seemed the police were there in minutes. Amanda and I explained our version of events to officers. When they separated us, I went into detail about my day and my conversation with Drew. I told the cop, a light skinned black man, named Officer Hudgins, that I had been to the park earlier in the day with Mrs. Hawkins, and that a skater named Drew had harassed us. I told him I went to the restroom, and that when I returned, Mrs. Hawkins was gone. I then went and got Amanda to help me find her. We decided to retrace my steps, starting at the park. I told him that when we returned to the park, Amanda and some manly looking girl named Sarah, began to argue. When I started toward them to break it up, the aforementioned Drew stepped in front of me and stopped my progress. He told me to let them work it out on their own. I disagreed and forced my way past him. It was during this close contact that Drew must have pick-pocketed the van keys from me. I told Officer Hudgins that after I returned from a short walk with Amanda, the van and everything else was gone. He thanked me for my help, apologized for my loss, and then asked if I remembered anything else? I looked at the ground. After a moment of what I hoped passed for deep concentration, I looked up. "Yeah, there is something else…I think he said something about McDonald Forest."

MONDAY 10:37 A.M.

I enjoyed my Monday mornings. The upside to working 40 hours in a weekend was hearing the world go back to work Monday morning. While they drank coffee to stay awake, I laid in bed smelling Amanda on my pillows. Her scent was sweet and dry, like a desert with candy canes. I didn't know if we'd ever hook up again, but I did know she stuck her neck out for me last night. After the police came, and before they found Drew and Sarah at McDonald Forest, Amanda and I went back to Harrington's and explained what happened. Now Amanda could have told the truth and hung me out to dry. I mean in all honesty, she was innocent of any wrongdoing, but she didn't do that. Instead, she confirmed my lie. She told our manager that

I had permission to take Mrs. Hawkins out -that part was true- but everything else was bullshit. She wasn't there when Mrs. Hawkins was "taken" from Bryant Park. Nor had she seen me fight off the theft of the van, but that didn't stop her from saying she had. Her lies were obviously an attempt at getting revenge on Sarah. I didn't know how to feel about that. Part of me was more than happy to see her spite benefit me; however, another part of me was amazed at the level of her revenge. I hate cheaters too, but I don't think I could pin a murder charge on someone as payback. But seeing the sticky situation I was in, and not wanting to be judgmental (or go to jail), I decided to keep my objections to myself.

I rolled out of bed and continued thinking about the previous night. I couldn't believe what had happened. I had accidentally killed Mrs. Hawkins, Drew and Sarah had taken the rap for it, and I was being praised as a hero at work for defending Mrs. Hawkins with all my might- something that had never happened. Crazy! I stood naked in front of my bedroom window and put on a pair of athletic shorts. I didn't know who now lived in the apartment behind me, but I figured they deserved a right to see my sexiness in its full glory… unless they were a dude. In that case, they were just gay. And even if that were the case, I'd continue to give them a show. Attention is attention.

I walked in the living room and saw Moose standing by the back door. Old reliable, Moose. He had no idea of last night's events.

I opened the door and let him out. He jogged into the backyard and did his routine: sniff, spin, shit. Watching him do what he had done a thousand times before soothed me. It made me think everything was still the same. I grabbed a bowl of cereal and headed to the shower.

While shampooing my hair, I heard my cell phone receive two separate calls. Either two people were thinking about me at almost the same time, or someone was really trying to get a hold of me. I hopped out of the shower and went in the bedroom. After dressing in front of the window once more, I grabbed my cell phone off the nightstand. The calls were from a number I didn't recognize. I put the phone in my pocket and headed for the living room. As I walked down the hallway, I faintly heard voices and wondered if I had left the TV on. I realized I hadn't when I saw Sean and Rachel sitting on my couch. Both were true to form with Rachel wearing a black and white polka dot dress with black four-inch heels, and Sean, not to be outdone, sporting a pair of tight, turquoise jeans with a long-sleeved purple shirt buttoned up halfway. His sleeves, for more range of motion, were folded to his elbows, naturally. At least his collar wasn't propped up.

"What the hell are you two doing here, Jiop Lin?" I asked. "How'd you get inside?"

Choosing to ignore my Jiop Lin comment, Rachel sat up straight and smiled. "I have key you know," she said. "We come by see you."

"You come by see me, Rachel? Why you come by see me? And why'd you bring this douchebag with you?" I asked pointing at Sean.

"Hey, look, asshole," interrupted Sean, "I'm only here because Rachel asked me to come, okay? So fuck off!"

"Oh, you supposed to be her protection?" I asked sarcastically. "How'd that work out for you last time?" Sean stood up from the couch.

"Lucky punch," he replied.

"Lucky punch? I knocked you out! You were unconscious in my front lawn!"

"Doesn't make it any less of a lucky punch," he answered. "Just means you got lucky and connected."

I was in awe of his denial. "What?" I shrieked. "You're like 5" 3' there's no wa…"

"I'm 5" 6', asshole!"

"Whatever," I said laughing. "It's like fighting a retarded middle schooler. Or a blind newborn kitten! There's no way you…"

"Stop it now!" Rachel screamed. "Shut up both you!" Sean and I stopped arguing, glared at each other, and then focused on Rachel. "Look," she said, "I come here tell you I heard what happened to old lady you with at park yesterday. She die. I saw."

I nervously laughed her comment off. "What do you mean you saw?" I asked. "She was found in a lake up in McDonald Forest. How'd you see that?"

"Nooo! Nooo!" Rachel said, wagging a finger in front of her face. "She fall out chair. Hit head. I saw. Bust her shit wide open."

I was shocked into silence. "Did you just say, *bust her shit wide open*? You been watching BET or something, Rachel?" I walked past the couch, through the living room, and let Moose back inside. He instantly ran to Rachel. "I don't know what to tell ya," I continued. "Mrs. Hawkins was alive after she fell. Besides, I already told the police everything that happened, so I don't know why you're here. What do you want?"

Rachel pushed Moose aside and stood up from the couch. "I tell you what I want," she said, but she didn't get a chance. Before she could say anything else, there was a knock at the front door. As I went to answer it, I wondered who would be knocking on my door at 11 in the morning. My day, less than an hour old, had already started terribly, and I had a feeling it was only going to get worse. Standing on my front step was Toucan with a concerned expression.

MONDAY 11:09 A.M.

"What are you doing here, Toucan? How do you know where I live?" He swayed gently and rubbed his hair.

"I've got to talk to you, man," he said. "I'm freaking out, bro!"

I asked Rachel and Sean to excuse me and stepped out the front door. "What are you talking about," I asked, "and how the hell do you know where I live?" My questions obviously made no impact on him because he continued as if I had never asked them.

"You lied about that old lady," he said while looking at the ground. "You lied. Drew and Sarah didn't kill her; we did, didn't we?" He looked up at the end of his question. He was looking for the truth. He didn't know what to believe.

"What?" I began. "No. I mean, yes. I mean, no, we didn't kill her, yes, the skater kids, Drew and Amanda, did it. They killed her. Why do you think we killed her?" I asked. "And how do you know where I live?"

After listening to him ramble about various things, at various speeds, with various inflections, I cut him off. "Toucan," I interrupted, "you're not making any sense, and I'm in the middle of something right now." He stopped talking and looked at the ground again. He appeared to be having one of his lost days. Some days Toucan could be normal and only slightly strange, but other days, like today, he was hard to understand, let alone be around. "Go to Lumpy's," I continued. "When I finish here, I'll come straight to you, okay?" He nodded and mumbled something under his breath. Before I could ask him what he said, he turned and left the porch. I stepped back inside to deal with Sean and Rachel.

"Sorry about that," I said, closing the door behind me. "This day's already starting off crazy." I walked back into the living room and sat down on the edge of the coffee table.

"Who was at door?" Rachel asked.

"No one important," I said. "Now, what is it you two want?" Rachel and Sean exchanged confused expressions before answering my question. Rachel cleared her throat before speaking.

"I not know what going on," she said, "but I will figure out." She stood and told Sean to follow.

"So you're just gonna leave?" I asked, as they walked toward the door. Rachel opened the door and paused for a moment.

"I'll be back," she said before walking out. Sean followed behind her and shot me a glare over his shoulder. Moose rose and tried to follow them, but he was too slow. The door closed in his face.

I sat on the coffee table and tried to take in the morning's events. Running a hand across my face, I closed my eyes and mentally recapped the vital information. For starters, Rachel had seen Mrs. Hawkins fall from the wheelchair. That much was true. However, she didn't know, for a fact, that that fall is what killed Mrs. Hawkins. She just thought it suspicious that the same woman she saw face-plant in my care, was found dead in a lake shortly thereafter, and I had nothing to do with it. I felt my stomach drop as I followed her logic. It was sound. Hell, she had a pretty damn good case. I wouldn't believe my story either if I were her. As painful as that realization was, the shitty part was, she wasn't even my biggest problem; Toucan was.

I rose from the table and walked into the kitchen. A situation like this called for a clear mind, and I didn't know a better way to clear my mind than smoking a joint. I grabbed the cereal box off the fridge and emptied its contents. I still had nearly an ounce of weed left. Besides the stuff I had burned with Rachel, the bag was basically untouched. I grabbed some rolling papers from my nightstand and brought the cereal box to the coffee table.

Maury Povich was the background noise as I rolled a decent sized joint. I lit it with a book of matches I normally used for candles in the living room. They were the same candles I burned when Rachel would give me my one pity lay a month. Just because we only had sex once a month, didn't mean I couldn't set the mood. Candles and Marvin Gaye, that was our thing. Seeing her in that polka dot dress made me reminisce. She was something sexy, alright! As I smoked, I sat and thought about the good times Rachel and I had. My memories were first interrupted by the out-of-control teens on Maury, then by my cell phone. I took another hit, then reached in my pocket. When I looked at the number, I noticed it was the same one that had called twice when I was in the shower. I exhaled a cloud of smoke and answered, "Hello..."

MONDAY 11:32 A.M.

There was silence on the other end of the phone. "Hello?" I repeated. There was a muffled noise in response. I waited a little longer and was about to hang up when a woman's voice finally answered.

"Hello," she said. "Can you hear me?"

"Yeah, I can hear you. Who is this?"

"It's Martha. You got a minute?" I exhaled slightly and wiped my face with my hand.

"Actually, Martha, I'm a little busy at the moment. Can I give you a call back a little later?" She asked me not to hang up and kept repeating how "important" it was I came into work. "Do they need me to cover someone's shift?" I asked in response.

"No," she said, "it's nothing like that." She slowly took a breath and continued. "I wanted to talk to you about your dog, Moose."

"Moose," I said. "You wanna talk to me about Moose? Why, Martha?" I hurried and changed clothes as she spoke. She told me that she remembered the conversation I had had with her about Moose. She remembered me telling her that he could help her. And with events like last night, she realized life is short, and anytime is the right time to change one's perspective.

I think she expected me to have an emotional connection with her words, but I was concentrating on tying my Nikes. I heard what she was saying, and I recalled telling her Moose could help her, but I didn't have time for that. I had to find Toucan.

"You're right," I said. "It's tragic what those kids did to Mrs. Hawkins." I steadied my voice for my next comment. "And to be honest, I can't help but blame myself. I should have been there for her!" I paused so Martha could hear me pound the top of my dresser for dramatic effect. "She was too young, Martha, too young."

"What are you talking about?" asked Martha. "She was over eighty years-old."

"Young at heart, Martha. She was young at heart." I cleared my throat and told her I really needed to go. "If you still want to talk about Moose tomorrow, I'm available all day, but I've really got to go right now."

"But it's really important," she said. "If you just stop by…"

"Can't do it today, Martha. Sorry." And with that, I hung up on her in mid-sentence. I kissed Moose on the head and raced out the door to meet Toucan at Lumpy's.

MONDAY 11:51 A.M.

I never made it a habit of frequenting bars before noon, so when I walked inside Lumpy's, I didn't know what to expect. The bartender working was Lance. Lance was a quiet white guy with glasses and a thin build. He looked more like a computer geek than a bartender.

The good thing about Lance was that he left the customers alone. He didn't try to get chatty with you. The bad thing about Lance was that he was extremely boring. He did everything by the book. No bar humor, no stiff drinks, and no discussion. He was the kind of guy you could sit next to for hours, day after day, and have no memory of ever meeting the guy. I assumed that's why he worked the day shift. People who get drunk by noon don't need to remember anything.

I headed to Toucan's normal location, (last seat, far end of the bar) and found him nursing a pint. Surrounding him were other local rejects, Lumpy's staff members, and two businessmen who looked entirely out of place. Toucan saw me enter and stood up from his stool. He started toward me, but realizing he had forgotten his beer, turned back suddenly to grab it. When he had turned back around, I was standing in front of him.

"What do you need to talk about, Toucan? What's so important?"

His response to my questions was to take a gulp from his glass and belch.

"Excuse me," he said. "Sorry about that." His burp smelled like peanuts, beer, and gingivitis. A potpourri I truly hoped to never smell again.

"Come on," I said, grabbing his arm and leading him to a table in the rear. He appeared more controlled than he was at my front door. Either he had gotten a hold of himself, or he was drunk?

With his mood swings, it was hard to tell. "What do you want to talk about?" I asked again as we sat down. "What's so important I had to come here and meet you?" Toucan shifted in his seat a few seconds before he spoke.

"How's your dog doing?" he asked before anything else.

"My dog is fine, Toucan. Thanks for asking. Now, what do you need to talk about?"

"What's his name? Mouse...or...Moses...or...?"

"Moose," I said, "my dog's name is Moose."

"Moose, that's right. He's a pretty dog, man."

"Damn it, Toucan! I really hope you didn't have me come down here to talk about my fucking dog! What's the problem?" My words seemed to sting because he became quiet and looked at me coldly.

"You have to tell me one thing," he asked. "Did we kill that old lady?"

"Damn it, Toucan, I've already answered this! No! No, we did not kill Mrs. Hawkins. Those damn skater punks did. I told you that then, and I told you that when you came to my house. And you still haven't told me how you know where I live!"

"It doesn't matter how I know where you live," he answered. "It's like asking why a river flows to the sea; it just does, and it doesn't matter, because you can't change it."

"What the hell are you talking about, Toucan? I ne..."

"Besides," he continued, "that's not what I need to talk to you about." He took a slow drink from his pint glass. "I don't believe you. I don't think Drew and Sarah killed that old lady. I think we did. Now why you wanted to kill that old woman and play with her nipple is beyond me."

"I told you, there was a fly on her nipple!" I interrupted. "Stop trying to make me sound like some sicko."

He brushed my comment aside as if juvenile. "Whatever the case," he said, "I can't let two innocent people go to jail for what we did."

My hands suddenly became moist and my heart began to beat double time. I was afraid he could see it pounding through my shirt.

"What exactly are you trying to say, Toucan?"

He took another drink from his pint glass. "I'm saying I'm going to the police." My stomach panged. "And if you have a conscience," he added, "you'll do the same thing."

It took me a second to digest what Toucan was telling me, and that worked out perfectly because he needed a second to finish his beer. He set his glass back on the table and waited for my response.

"Why?" I asked. "Why turn yourself in for something you didn't do? How are you so sure Drew and Sarah didn't kill her?"

"Because I've been buying weed from Drew for almost two years!" Toucan answered. "I think I know him well enough to know if he could do something like that."

"Really?" I asked in a mocking tone. "Buying weed from someone gives you an accurate assessment of someone's character or moral fiber? That's ridiculous, Toucan! It's like saying you can see motherly instincts in a prostitute you've been using for over a year! Absolutely retarded!" Toucan seemed unaffected by my comments. He only smiled and shrugged his shoulders.

"Say what you want," he said, "I can only tell you what I know. And what I know is Drew's an asshole, but he ain't a killer. We killed that old lady."

For the next twenty minutes we argued who was responsible for Mrs. Hawkins' death, and how to deal with that information. The whole conversation was pointless because Toucan was adamant about turning himself in. I couldn't talk him out of it. He stopped short of demanding I do the same. He said he could understand if I didn't want to turn myself in, seeing as I had Moose to take care of.

"I don't have anyone at home waiting for me," he said in a sad voice. "You do. You need to take care of Moose. He's such a handsome dog! I can't, in good conscience, ask you to abandon him. I'll take the wrap."

So there it was. Toucan, in what I'm sure was a drunken stupor, had volunteered to take a murder charge for Mrs. Hawkins' death. And he was doing this out of some perverse respect for Moose, a dog he had only met the day before. I wasn't sure what to say. This was an extremely kind gesture. It was also completely insane, but I figured I should respect his wishes. I mean who was I to attempt talking him out of his plan? The least I could be was supportive.

"Wow, Toucan...I don't know what to say. Moose would thank you." I stood up from the table and straightened my clothes. "At least let me buy you a drink before you turn yourself in."

"Thanks," said Toucan. We started back to the bar, before he stopped and faced me. "If it's not too much trouble," he asked in a polite voice, "could you drop me off at the police station after we're finished here?"

"You still only turning yourself in?" I asked without thinking.

"Yeah," he responded. "Why do you ask?"

"No reason," I said. "No reason at all." I placed my hand on his shoulder and guided him back toward the bar. "I'll take you to turn yourself in, Toucan. It would be my pleasure. But first, let's get you a drink!"

MONDAY 2:27 P.M.

Watching Toucan turn himself in was a surreal sight. There was a part of me that respected his morals, his conscience. I was impressed because I had stopped listening to mine years ago. I felt somewhat responsible for Toucan's surrender, but quickly reminded myself that no man can truly make another man *do* anything, so my guilt was short-lived. He walked in through the glass doors with his hands raised above his head. I was obviously too far away to hear the words his lips mouthed, but I assumed they had something to do with murder, because after he said them, an officer rushed over and pinned him on the ground. As more officers rushed to assist in Toucan's arrest, I decided my job was done and it was time to get going. Now that Toucan was taken care of, it was time to deal with everyone else, starting with Martha.

MONDAY 2:53 P.M.

On the drive to Harrington's my cell phone rang three times. One of the calls was from Martha; the other two were from a private number. I didn't answer Martha's call because I was already on my way to Harrington's, and I'd rather speak to her face to face. I didn't answer the private number because it was private. The only people who ever called from private numbers were telemarketers and assholes, which are damn near the same thing, and I didn't have time to talk to either.

When I got to Harrington's, I parked in the side lot and casually entered the building. The first floor was its usual self; busy and bustling. Active seniors were watching television, walking back and forth; basically looking like a pamphlet cover page. I crossed this scene unnoticed as I headed to the elevator. When the elevator doors opened Mr. Rash was waiting for me inside.

"About time you showed up," he said with his arms folded across his chest.

"What are you doing?" I asked.

"Waiting for you," he responded. "I wanted to be the first face you saw when you got here." I stepped inside the elevator and pressed the floor number. "Been in here almost two hours," he said with a smile.

"You've been waiting in this elevator for two hours, Mr. Rash?" I laughed slightly under my breath. "How'd you even know I was coming in? I'm not scheduled to work today."

"I know," he said, "Martha called you in." The elevator doors opened and I followed him out. He turned around and smirked at me. "Didn't think I knew, did you?" he asked. "You'd be surprised what I know." He jerked his head over his right shoulder and told me to follow him. He said Martha was waiting for me in the cafeteria. We walked silently down the hallways and I wondered why Martha would tell Mr. Rash she wanted to talk to me. What did he have to do with anything?

When we entered the cafeteria, Martha was sitting in the middle and it was oddly empty. Usually there were a few seniors sitting around looking out a window, or playing a game of bridge, but not today. There was no one else in there except a few staff members cleaning up in the kitchen. I sat down across the round table from Martha. Mr. Rash stood behind me. For such an old man, he sure could stand for extended periods of time.

"You sure you don't want to sit, Mr. Rash?" I asked without turning my head around. "All that standing in the elevator probably made you a little tired, right"

"Oh, no, I'm good," he responded. "I like the view." I shook my head and focused back on Martha.

"So...what's up? Why'd you want me to come in here and see you?" Martha smiled with an air of disbelief.

"Well let's see," she said. "Maybe I wanted to talk about what happened yesterday? Does that sound reasonable to you?

I pretended to give the question a good going over before finally responding.

"Yeah," I said in a grave tone. "Yeah, that sounds fair."

Martha rolled her eyes and looked at Mr. Rash. "Just listen," she said. "I knew nothing good would come out of your little trip, that's why I called in sick. You didn't know that did you?"

"No, Martha, I didn't know that."

"Shut up," she responded. "I'm not finished. I hoped you'd decide not to go after I called in sick, but it didn't work; you went anyway. Luckily, Mr. Rash and I know you well, so we were prepared for you. I knew there was a chance you'd try to have your little field trip anyway, so Mr. Rash was kind enough to personally persuade everyone else not to go with you. We even put a tag on the van stating the engine needed service. I thought that about covered the bases. I felt safe your little field trip was over, but I was wrong. Not only did you still have your little field trip, you took Mrs. Hawkins with you! These actions were not only stupid beyond description, they ultimately cost Mrs. Hawkins her life!" Martha stopped talking and stared at me with her hands on her hips.

"I mean...if you want something...you've gotta go after it," I said, feeling she wanted an explanation of some sort.

"You're unbelievable!" snapped Martha. Mr. Rash echoed her sentiments with a contemptuous snort.

"Well, what do you want me to say?" I blurted. "Do you think I planned for this to happen? You think I knew someone would kidnap and kill Mrs. Hawkins? I'm sorry for what happened, but it was truly out of my control!" I buried my face in my hands and breathed heavily. I waited for a response from either of them but heard nothing. After a moment, I lifted my face from my hands and looked at Martha. She looked unimpressed.

"Are you finished?" she asked in a facetious tone. "I don't know what happened to Mrs. Hawkins at the skatepark," she continued, "but I wouldn't be surprised to find out you were involved."

I acted shocked and appalled at her statement. "Why would you say such a..."

"Stop," she said, interrupting me. "Just stop. I'm tired of your stories. We're going to fix this issue once and for all, you understand?"

I nodded silently as if by instinct.

"Great," she said. "Now, like I was saying, you probably had something to do with Mrs. Hawkins' death, in fact I'd bet on it, but what concerns me more, is that I'm indirectly involved in all this. You came to me with the plans for this trip, and stupidly I didn't tell management. Therefore, I could get caught up in this shit also. So for the protection of my own ass, my own ass, we're going to help you out of this mess."

"We?" I asked in confusion.

"Yes, we." She answered. "Mr. Rash and I are going to help you get out of this sticky situation. And we're only going to ask for three little things in return."

I sat quietly pivoting my stare from Martha to Mr. Rash, and back again. I spoke to Martha in a cautious tone while looking at Mr. Rash. "And what three things are those?" I asked.

MONDAY 3:21 P.M.

The most interesting thing about vomiting, to me anyway, has always been that while puking can definitely make you feel better, you have to go through a small amount of pain to receive the relief vomiting grants you. The sweating, mouthwatering, and bitter bile taste are all temporary pains one must endure in order to enjoy the benefits of puking. Now even though most people agree they feel better after throwing up, they still despise the act. This conflict of emotions is natural and explains why we often need encouragement to vomit. We need someone to tell us that the pain is only temporary, and the outcome justifies the means. This was essentially the same concept Martha was using in dealing with me. She promised to smooth the whole "Mrs. Hawkins murder thing" over with management on my behalf, and Mr. Rash vowed to unite the residents in support of me. That would be the relief part of this puking scenario. Martha kept encouraging me to focus on that part. "It's for the best," she repeated over and over. And what did I have to do? What pain did I have to endure to get this relief? Just three simple things.

The first step in the deal required me quitting my job at Harrington's. Martha said it would look better that way. She said quitting would give the impression that Mrs. Hawkins' death had really shaken me. That way no one would suspect me of any involvement. And Mr. Rash added his belief that everyone at Harrington's would be happier without me around. I hated him so much!

Next, Martha wanted me to give her Moose. She said she had thought about all the things I had said about Moose, about him changing my life, and how he made me happy. She felt she needed some more happiness in her life. She also said if I didn't give her Moose, she would tell Harrington's management about my fetish with Mrs. Hawkins' sponge baths. I told her I took umbrage with the term "fetish" being tossed around, and that I believed there was mutual enjoyment during Mrs. Hawkins' sponge baths. "The woman knew she was a specimen for her age!" I explained. Martha didn't appear to share my opinion, which didn't surprise me. Women are always jealous of one another.

The final request came from Mr. Rash. He told me he'd get the other residents to speak well of me, and the trip I took Mrs. Hawkins on, if I'd do one thing for him- give him my guitar. He said he was tired of Mr. Corbit "strutting around like he was hot stuff" with his guitar. It made him crazy watching Mr. Corbit play songs for staff members and residents. Said he didn't like showoffs, and that's exactly what Mr. Corbit was. Therefore, he wanted a guitar himself. That way Mr. Corbit couldn't feel as unique or special. I wanted to tell him his plan was extremely vindictive and childish but figured the words would go to waste. Instead, I looked at it as another example of why I hated him so much...such a dick!

So there it was. My potential freedom could be secured by simply surrendering my job, my dog, and my guitar. I sat motionless thinking of what to say. They were driving a tough bargain. The job they could have, but my guitar and dog too?

"I'm gonna have to think about this," I said and rose from the table.

"Just where are you going?" Martha asked.

"I need to think," I answered and walked away from the table. I headed for the exit and looked back over my shoulder.

"You've got till noon tomorrow," she yelled after me. If I don't hear from you by then, I'm going straight to management!"

MONDAY 4:15 P.M.

Moose was on the couch when I came home. He didn't get up to greet me anymore. Time had definitely changed our relationship, but I still loved him. He was the only person (even though he's not a person) that I truly trusted. Unfortunately, it was obvious we were drifting apart. Seeing me used to be the highlight of his day. Now we simply coexisted. I shook my head as I thought about this and let him out the back door. Why did Martha want to take him from me? She had never met Moose. How could she be so sure he'd help her? I grew angry as I pondered the question. However, another part of me asked a different question. A voice inside my mind wondered how Moose would feel. What would he want? Would he object to receiving a new home? Did he also feel we had drifted apart? I poured some food in his bowl and grabbed the weed out of the cereal box. If I was going to make such a serious decision, I thought it wise to be as open-minded as possible.

I smoked the joint on the couch while watching Moose smell shit in the backyard. He never ran out of things to smell. Occasionally he'd smell something unpleasant and shake his head before sneezing. It was a good and simple life he had. Watching all of this made me wonder, do dogs have regret? Is that an emotion they they're capable of feeling? I mean one wouldn't think so, but what if they do? What if they can't smell that last bush they want to smell because their owner pulls them away? How long does that bush not smelled linger in their mind? My thought was interrupted with the ringing of my doorbell. Caught off guard, I rushed to put the joint out, fanned the room with my arms, and headed to the door. It was Amanda.

"We need to talk," she said while shoving her way through the door.

"Come on in," I said sarcastically while closing the door.

"Ohh! Looks like I came at the perfect time," she said before taking the joint out of the ashtray and grabbing my lighter. I sat across from her on the couch and watched her take a few hits. She was one of those smokers who takes the biggest hit her lungs can possibly hold. While this may make sense on the surface, get all you can get, it's highly unappealing to the observer. Amanda would cough and wheeze after every hit. Her face would turn red and a vein throbbed on the side of her forehead. It was an ugly thing to witness. If I didn't smoke already, her hacking and watering eyes would make me think twice about beginning the habit.

"What do we need to talk about, Amanda?" She took one last drag from the joint and exhaled. She coughed so hard she had to spit. She walked to my kitchen sink and let a few drops of phlegm slide down the drain, and then she got a glass of tap water. Did she really just spit a loogie down my sink, I thought to myself? I started to wonder how I found this slob attractive enough to have sex with. Then I remembered how nice her breasts were and stopped asking myself such stupid questions. "You okay?" I asked. She finished her glass of water before speaking.

"I need a drink," she said without looking at me. "Let's go to that shitty bar of yours."

MONDAY 4:39 P.M.

When we got to Lumpy's, I was again disappointed to see Garrett bartending. It was like he lived there or something. Every day I went there hoping it would be his day off, and every day he'd be there to greet me with his smug face. I couldn't stand him.

"Hey, I thought I suspended you?" Garret remarked as I walked past the bar.

"I thought I suspended you?" I mocked in a high-pitched voice without looking at him. Obviously sensing my resentment, Amanda grabbed our drinks and met me at the far corner table. She sat our drinks down and stared at me, waiting for me to finish a statement I had abandoned mid-sentence.

"What?" I asked somewhat annoyed.

"Are you going to tell me what happened?" she asked.

"About what?"

She shook her head and took a long drink from her glass. "Are you serious?" she asked with a sarcastic chuckle. "Are you fucking serious? Mrs. Hawkins is found dead in a lake, and you don't know what I'm asking you about?" She resumed her pensive stare at me.

"Wait…you think I had something to do with her death?" I waited for her denial of my accusation. She didn't offer one. "Just what are you trying to imply, Amanda?"

She rolled her eyes and finished her pint in an impressive single gulp. "I'm trying to imply," she began, "that you had something to do with Mrs. Hawkins' death. I don't know how you're involved, but I know you're involved, and I'm not going to help you until you first admit it, and then do me a favor!" She finished her statement with a burp.

I couldn't help but notice a pattern developing. Everyone suspected I was involved with Mrs. Hawkins' death, but they had no proof, and to stop them from voicing their inclinations to the authorities, I had to jump through some stupid hoop. Mr. Rash wanted my guitar. Martha wanted my job and my dog. I could only imagine what Amanda wanted. A kidney? An overseas adoption? Some frozen sperm? The last one didn't seem too crazy for some reason. Perhaps there was still some chemistry between us? I decided it wise to feel her out a little more- no pun intended.

"Fine, Amanda, I'll bite. If I were involved, which I'm not saying I was, why would I need your help, and most importantly, what would I have to give to get it?"

"Well," she began, "you need my help because I was with you yesterday at the park. I'm the closest thing you have to an alibi. I can vouch for your whereabouts...and whatnot"

"Okay," I said in the best unimpressed voice I could muster. "I see where you're going with this, so..."

"What is it I want?" she interrupted. "It's simple- silence. All I want is silence." I looked at her bewildered.

"Silence? I don't get it."

"It's really not that difficult to *get*." She gave me a snide look and got up and headed to the bar. When she returned, she was carrying two shots. "Drink this," she said. It was tequila. I hated tequila.

"I want silence," she continued. "I want you to promise you'll never tell anyone we had sex. No one can EVER know!" She took her shot and wiped her lips with her forearm, looking at me the entire time. "Can you do that for me?" she asked.

Having never been asked such a question, I didn't know what to say. Hell, I didn't even know how to take it. My pride was hurt. Before I jumped to any conclusions, I asked her for clarification.

"So you want to wait until everything cools down before word gets out about us, is that what you're saying?" She looked at me like I was crazy.

"No," she said slowly, "I'm not waiting for anything to cool down. I'm embarrassed. I don't want anyone to ever know, ever, that I had sex with you. Is that clear enough? *Do* you *get it* now?" She was staring at me again waiting for a response. I knew she was trying to be stern with me, but her pale skin and freckles contradicted her attitude. Her auburn hair made her look like a nymph from The Odyssey, and I once again thought about her perky breasts.

"Hello!" She interrupted my meditation. "Are you even listening to me?" I snapped back to reality and assessed the situation.

"Yes, Amanda, I'm listening to you, but I don't know what to tell you. It…it kind of hurts my feelings. I thought we had something or were at least working our way toward something. Was that just me?" I asked. "Was I the only one feeling that?"

"Yes," she responded, "you were definitely the only one feeling that. So do we have a deal or not?"

"Really? You don't feel anything? You didn't enjoy it?"

"Do we have a deal or not?" she repeated in a flat voice.

"Fine," I said slightly embarrassed, "we have a deal. I won't tell anyone we had sex."

"Thank you," she said. "Now, tell me what happened with Mrs. Hawkins…and be honest! Tell me the truth!"

"Alright, I will. But first…" I grabbed the shot of tequila and swallowed it as fast as I could, grimacing as it burned its way down my throat… "we're gonna need more of these!"

MONDAY 5:55 P.M.

The truth is such a subjective term, and alcohol is such a social lubricant, that Amanda heard the best summary I considered safe to tell her. My story hardly changed. I told her Drew and Sarah had indeed killed Mrs.

Hawkins, and I made no mention of Toucan. The new wrinkle I added was that I let Drew and Sarah use the van to dump Mrs. Hawkins' body. When she asked why I did that, I told her they gave me the weed that nearly made her cough up a lung at my house earlier. That was their payment for using the van. Being a stoner, she asked no more questions about it. In fact, "You might have gotten the better end of that deal." she added with a laugh. We left Lumpy's and headed back to my house. I repeated my version of Mrs. Hawkins' death numerous times on the drive. Each time I added a little more to imply that I was simply a victim of circumstances. In the wrong place at the wrong time, but everything had worked out fine because Drew and Sarah were now in custody for killing Mrs. Hawkins. I had taken the long way to justice, but we had arrived there, nonetheless. She agreed and was appearing to feel much better about me. Gone was the doubt and anger in her eyes as I told my story. She had expected to hear the worst from me, but instead had heard a rational explanation. Now her eyes were filled with apologies and alcohol- a beautiful combination. I was planning to sleep with her again. We would go inside my house, smoke another joint, and have sex once more. But this time she was going to like it. This time I would use my "special" move. I was confident, borderline arrogant as we turned onto my street. Amanda believed I was innocent in a murder case, and she was about to believe I was good in bed, too. What else could you want in life? I was free of suspicion and guilty of seduction. That would make a nice tattoo or a good bumper sticker, I thought to myself. People would buy that wouldn't they? Whether they would or wouldn't was irrelevant. What was important was that I had just found my post-orgasm conversation topic.

MONDAY 9:14 P.M.

I've always been a deep sleeper, especially when drunk and trying to forget a forgettable sexual performance; but even sober I slept hard. There were train tracks that ran through my backyard as a child. The trains would switch tracks, connect carts, and blow horns all night behind my house. Whenever friends would stay over, they would complain about how they couldn't sleep with all the noise in the backyard. I never heard a sound. The older I got, the only surefire way to wake me up was either by physical contact or screaming. Those were hard for me to tune out, especially barks like Moose's and screams like Amanda's.

A little after nine, I awoke to Moose barking and Amanda screaming like a toddler. When I finally pieced together what was going on, I asked her what was the matter. She said there was someone outside the window watching her sleep, and she was getting the hell out of there. She got up and quickly started getting dressed. She was thin and pale. I liked the way my skin looked pressed against her white skin. It made me look darker. Blacker. I didn't like her figure, skinny with no ass, but I did like how petite she was. It made me feel strong. Manly. She buttoned her pants and put her shirt on. She didn't wear a bra. There was no reason to; her boobs were that nice!

"Are you just going to lay there?" she asked in anger. I got up and put on a robe.

"Calm down," I said. "I'll go check it out. Wait for me in the living room." I searched for my shoes, and after finding them, I followed her into the living room. She was sitting on the couch scanning the room like a deer before drinking water. "I'll be right back, okay?"

"I'm not staying in here alone," she said.

"What? Why?"

"Because I don't feel safe here!"

"Okay…" I tried to think of a compromise. "Do you want to look for the guy outside with me?" She didn't even entertain my question.

"I'm going home!" she said sternly and started walking toward the front door.

"You're gonna walk home alone after dark? Seriously?"

"It's better than being here!" she snapped. Seeing how upset she was becoming, I decided it wise to take control of the situation.

"Amanda!" She stopped at the door. "Stop being a bitch and wait for me to check outside the house." I gave her a strong glare that expressed I was in control. "I'm not gonna let anything happen to you." Apparently unfazed by my statement, Amanda grabbed the doorknob and looked back over her shoulder.

"Nice try," she said, "but I'm going home anyway. And by the way, your bumper sticker or tee shirt, whatever idea is stupid!" She half walked, half ran across my lawn to the sidewalk.

"Low class, Amanda. Low class…" I echoed after her.

I tightened my robe and walked to the back of the house. My backyard was small and unless they could fit in a trash can under a lawnmower or in a pile of dog shit, there weren't many places for a burglar to hide. "Anyone back there?" I called from the fence's edge. "Hello?" I waited a couple seconds and heard nothing. Just as I was deciding to call again or walk back inside, a figure stood up from behind the trash can.

"Hey, bro." the voice said. Startled, I stepped back and tried to focus on the figure. It looked oddly familiar.

"Toucan? What the hell are you doing out here? Why aren't you in jail?"

"They sent me home, bro. Sorry to interrupt your night, I didn't have anywhere else to go." I walked back to the front of the house and looked for Amanda in the streetlights. She was almost out of eyesight now. Toucan walked up behind me.

"Don't worry about it, bro. She'll cool down in a couple days. She always does."

"What are you talking about, Toucan, you don't even know her." I turned around and found Toucan with an embarrassed look on his face.

"That was Amanda, right?" he asked in a soft voice.

I was shocked. "How'd you know that?"

Toucan let out a sigh of relief and patted his chest. "Oh, Man. Almost made a fool of myself, huh?"

"How'd you know her name?" I asked again.

"We used to mess around," he said. "She always throws a fit about something stupid."

I couldn't believe what I was hearing. Toucan and Amanda used to "mess around" with each other? What? He was nearly twenty years older than her, and homeless? How in the hell did this happen? Did I need to get an STD check?

"But on the upside," he continued, "she loves makeup sex, right?"

My face must have shown the horror I found in his words, because he stopped talking immediately. I pulled myself together and asked as calmly as I could, "You had sex with Amanda?"

He cleared his throat before responding. "I did, but it was nothing serious." We stood silently for a moment. "Doesn't she have great boobs?"

"Yeah, her boobs are great-...wait, why were you peeping in my window, Toucan? What's your problem?"

"Well I didn't mean to, man. You don't have any curtains, it's kind of like you wanted me to see."

"Toucan...you can't...it's not...well, actually that's a pretty good argument. It's still really creepy though, okay? Not cool!"

"Yeah, totally, bro. I get it. Not trying to creep you out." We stared at each other again in silence for a moment. "But seriously though, you should probably get that mole checked out on your back, bro. It's got an awkward shape and the edges looked kind of raised. So, for whatever it's worth..."

"Thanks, Toucan. Now please shut the hell up and get inside the house!"

"You got it, bro."

MONDAY 9:37 P.M.

I searched the fridge for something to eat while Toucan petted Moose. I needed to go grocery shopping. All I could find was a half empty, freezer burned pint of mint chocolate chip ice cream. It tasted old and rubbery, but I had the munchies, so it was better than tolerable to me. Toucan finished petting Moose before joining me in the living room. He casually flipped channels as he told me about his release from prison. He said they released him for lack of evidence. They said he was some nut-job looking for a few minutes of fame. Held him in a cell for a couple hours to let him sober up, and then sent him on his way. When I asked if he had said anything to the police about me or my involvement in Mrs. Hawkins' death, Toucan didn't respond. I began to worry, but then relaxed when I saw his delay wasn't from my question, but rather because he was focused on the television. His attention was being stolen by a documentary on the lives of seahorses.

"Toucan! Did you say anything to them about me?"

"What? They haven't talked to you yet?"

"No, not since the park. If they had, do you think I'd be asking you the questions I'm asking you?"

He paused for a second to ponder my question then said, "Oh, no, I guess you wouldn't, huh? Anyway, it's cool, bro, you're safe. They totally think Drew and Sarah did it."

I smiled at his news and felt a little more at ease. Maybe I wasn't going to get caught for this. Maybe I was really going to pull this off. The moment a smile was ready to curve my lips, I remembered the other side of the mess I was in. The police investigation may have been going my way, but I still had some problems to solve. I was guilty in the court of public opinion. What was I gonna do about Martha and Mr. Rash? Was it worth it to fight them? And what about Toucan, could I really trust someone as crazy as him to keep their mouth shut?

I decided to sleep on it. I told Toucan he could crash on the couch if he liked. He quickly accepted my offer of kindness and made himself at home. I locked the front door and headed for my room. "Did you really have sex with Amanda?" I asked before leaving the living room.

"Don't let that bother you, bro" he said. "It was like one or two times. Nothing big."

MONDAY 10:28 P.M.

I got in bed and thought about everything that had happened recently. Toucan was a trip. Why did he act crazy some days, and civilized others? And why hadn't he told the police about me? You could expect that type of loyalty from someone like Andy. He was a country person, and country people are simple. They value things like honesty, loyalty, and respect. They also value things like guns and a hatred for immigrants, but who's keeping track? People like Toucan were self-centered and not to be trusted, at least that's what I thought before he showed up at my house. Maybe he was a good, trustworthy type of guy? Don't get me wrong, he was still certifiably crazy, but it was a harmless, well-meaning type of crazy. He was off his rocker to help me dump Mrs. Hawkins' body for an ounce of weed, and he was absolutely insane for not ratting me out when he had the opportunity to do so. All I could do now was support his silence in my involvement. It's too bad Drew and Sarah were taking the fall for a crime they didn't commit, but come on, they were drug dealing douchebags. It's not like we lost a cure to world hunger with their incarceration.

I rolled onto my side and thought about tomorrow. I needed to give Martha and Mr. Rash a decision; time was running out. Martha worked tomorrow, and so did Amanda. Obviously, Mr. Rash would be there as well, so I decided to make a visit to Harrington's tomorrow some time. I laid in bed and looked out the window. I was getting tired. The day had been long and stressful, and I was still a little buzzed from all the drinking at Lumpy's. Tomorrow would be a better day. I closed my eyes and thought about Amanda and Toucan having sex. Then I thought of the unimpressive sex I had just had with Amanda. I wondered if she liked it more with Toucan. If she did, I couldn't blame her. It was like every time we did it, it got worse. She would never want to sleep with me again, and that bothered me. Not because I wouldn't be getting any ass anymore, but because I never got a "good one" in. There was nothing to stop her form saying sex with me was horrible. I could stand a woman not liking me, hell; she could hate me and regret having ever met me, but a woman not enjoying sex with me? That was hard to swallow. Slightly annoyed, I pulled the blankets up tight and fell asleep. I was going to need a clear, refreshed mind for the next day.

TUESDAY 8:09 A.M.

The sound of the back door opening and closing woke me up early. I had wanted to sleep later, but as with most things in life, I was getting accustomed to not getting my way. I got dressed and walked to the living room. Looking out the window I could see Toucan in the backyard with Moose.

"I think he wanted out," Toucan said as he reentered with Moose.

"That sounds about right. You hungry, Toucan? Want anything for breakfast?" He said he didn't want to bother me, and a piece of plain bread would do him fine.

"One piece of plain bread?" I asked somewhat in awe. "That's all you're gonna eat for breakfast?"

"I don't like to overeat," said Toucan. "I just need enough energy to get me to the next meal."

We ate at the kitchen table, something I rarely did. Toucan was telling me how he was going to change his life. How the last few days had been a sign from God to change his ways. He fed Moose a piece of his bread.

"It's like your dog calms me down. Makes me feel centered."

"Yeah, he does that," I said. Just as I was about to ask Toucan his plans for the day, my cell phone started ringing. I went to my bedroom to grab it, and saw it was Rachel calling. I decided to ignore it. I walked back in the living room where Toucan was once again petting Moose.

"Who was that?" he asked without looking up from petting Moose.

"Does it matter who it was, Toucan? Look, I need to get my day started, okay?" He looked up from Moose and got up from the table. "I'm not trying to be rude," I said. "I've just got a lot of shit to do today.

Nothing personal." I walked toward the front door and he followed behind me. Before he left, he turned and waved goodbye to Moose.

"It's cool," he said. "I have some things I should probably get to. See you later, bro." And with that he walked out of my house and across my driveway. It was kind of rude to kick Toucan out at eight in the morning, but he was the freeloading type. The type of guy who asks to crash on your couch for one night but ends up staying for three months. I had had enough of that in college. I didn't want to be mean to him, but I really did have a big day ahead of me.

I closed the door and looked at Moose. Toucan really liked Moose for some reason. I mean he was a handsome dog, but...? Staring at him and his wagging tail reminded me of all the things I had told Martha about him. About the way he could make you happy. About the way he simplified life. How he could help us become better people. I reached out and scratched his head. Even though the past week had been absolutely crazy, I still believed a lot of the things I told Martha about Moose. He did make me happy, and he could teach you to value the simple things in life. In short, I could see why she wanted him. Feeling our time coming to an end, I took Moose into the bedroom and climbed in the bed with him. He slept with me almost daily as a puppy, but soon grew too big and troublesome to sleep with the older he became. The couch was his bed now. My phone rang again, and I saw it was Rachel calling once more. There were more important things to deal with- Moose was leaving me. I didn't want to give him to Martha, but what was my other option? I mean I loved Moose, but I wasn't going down for murder and transporting a body, especially when Drew and Sarah were kind enough to take the fall for me. No thanks. Moose was great, but he had to go. I spooned him from behind and rubbed his side until I fell asleep, again. The day was a busy one, but not so busy I couldn't catch a nap with man's best friend.

TUESDAY 9:13 A.M.

Unable to keep Moose in the bed any longer, I accepted that the day had to begin. I walked to the back door and let Moose out. Maybe it was because Toucan let him out two hours earlier, but he didn't do his usual routine. There was no sniff, spin, and shit. Instead, he stood at the back door and looked at me. It was like he knew today would be a different day. He couldn't say as much verbally, but I could tell by his demeanor that he knew something was up. He was a special dog.

I left him outside and got dressed. Jeans and a faded blue shirt would do fine. As I sat on the edge of my bed and tied my shoes, the phone rang again. It was on the nightstand on the other side of the bed. Also on that side of the bed was my old guitar. I'd had it since college. The phone continued to ring. It was Rachel again. The third time she had called this morning. I didn't want to talk to her. She acted weird the last time I saw her. She had a bunch of questions about Mrs. Hawkins' death, and I didn't want to answer those right now. I set the phone on silent and put it in my pocket. Moose was ready to come in, and I was ready to go. I grabbed the guitar before I left the room.

Moose came back in and climbed up on the couch. I sat next to him and tuned my guitar while thinking about Mr. Rash and what an asshole he was. Life was funny. Nice, sweet, old people died every day, but assholes like Mr. Rash just kept on breathing.

The guitar was nothing special. It was an old electric acoustic I got on the west coast my sophomore year of college. I took it on camping trips and lugged it to every apartment or house I've lived in since. It had a nice sound, but it was nothing more than an expensive cheap guitar. I couldn't even remember what brand it was. Mr. Rash could actually do a lot better, but I wasn't going to tell him that. He could find that out on his own. Besides, I doubted he'd really care in the first place. He just wanted the guitar to spite Mr. Corbit. In a karma type of way, he deserved a shitty guitar.

I finished tuning Ol' Bertha, that's what I named the guitar in college, and started strumming a few chords. I hadn't played in months. My fingertips started to sting the longer I played, but I didn't care. This was probably the last time I'd play Ol' Bertha, so I was going to tough it out. I liked to play blues or reggae on the guitar. They were the two styles of music that fit my ear. It always felt to me that the guitar was made to play blues and reggae. There was just something mesmerizing to me about dirty blues licks, or rock steady reggae rhythms. I continued to play through cramps in my left hand. I was actually enjoying the impromptu jam session I was having with Moose on the couch. As the cramping became stronger, I wondered how much longer I could play. I decided to try for five more minutes. My fingertips and hand muscles began to burn, and I thought I heard something. Moose raised his head and got off the couch. I stopped playing. There was a knock on the front door. I put down the guitar and immediately thought of Rachel. She had already called me three times, so who else would it be? The only question was what did she want? You could never tell with her. I put Ol' Bertha down and opened the front door. Expecting to see Rachel, I was surprised to find a cop standing on my front steps. He was an older, light-skinned black man. He looked serious.

TUESDAY 9:28 A.M.

"May I come in, sir?" was all he said in response to my greeting.

"Uh, sure. Come on in." He followed me inside and I closed the door. Moose almost knocked him over before I could do anything to help. I pried Moose off and let him outside again. I quickly apologized and asked the officer to have a seat. He politely declined and continued standing. I couldn't put my finger on it, but something about him seemed familiar.

"My name is officer Hudgins," he said in a formal voice. "Do you know what I'm here to talk to you about?"

I walked to the couch and sat down. "I assume you have a few more questions about Mrs. Hawkins," I answered. He said I was correct and asked me to recite the day's events to him. When I told him I had already told the police everything at the park, he told me to "humor him." So I told him about going to work that day, and leaving for Bryant Park, and how Mrs. Hawkins and the van disappeared from in front of the restrooms, but he made me stop there. He kept asking about what happened when I first got to the park and how the van was stolen. Nothing else interested him. The weird thing was the more questions he asked, the more familiar his voice became. We spoke for at least a half-hour. I stuck to my story. Drew and Sarah took Mrs. Hawkins.

"Why'd they take her?" he asked.

"I don't know."

"How'd they get the keys to the van?"

"Couldn't tell you that either," I answered.

"Hmmm..."

Unable to contain my curiosity any longer, I finally asked, "Excuse me, Officer Hudgins, but you look familiar, have we ever met before or anything? Did I ever get a ticket from you or something?" He inhaled slightly and gripped his utility belt.

"Actually sir, we met a couple days ago at Bryant Park. I assisted you in loading Mrs. Hawkins into your company van." I felt a deep pang, and my mouth began to water.

"Oh, is that that's where I've seen you?" I chuckled lightly. "I knew we had met before." Officer Hudgins smiled politely before redirecting me back to his line of questioning. He asked, and I answered questions for the next 45 minutes. I kept wondering why he didn't take me down to the station to be interviewed, but I figured her knew what he was doing. Plus, as far as I was concerned, the longer I could avoid going to the police station; the better. He finished the interview by giving me his card and telling me to call him if I remembered anything new or had any questions. I shook his hand and walked him to the front door. He stopped short of the door and turned his attention to a picture on the end table.

"Those your parents?" he asked.

"Yeah," I responded. "That's mom and dad."

"Humph," he said with a smile. "Mine were the opposite."

"Yours were the opposite? I don't under-"

"My dad is white, and my mom is black, the opposite of yours."

"Oh, okay, I see what you're saying." We stood silently for a second. "Anyone ever think you're Hispanic?" I asked.

"No. Not that I know of. Why?"

"Because people always think I'm Hispanic, and it drives me crazy!"

"Really? That's stupid," said Officer Hudgins. "You don't look Hispanic to me." I smiled at his kind words. "You look more Latino than anything."

My smile disappeared instantly. "Thanks," I said, as sarcastically as possible. I opened the door for him to leave. "You have a good day now, Officer."

TUESDAY 10:37 A.M.

Officer Hudgins drove out of eyesight, and I stood on the porch for a moment. I didn't know what to make of him. Part of me wanted to embrace him as a fellow bi-racial man trying to avoid the dubious labels society insists on putting on us, while another part of me was terrified he was plotting my incarceration. I'd have to watch myself around him. Stay on my feet. Even though we were brethren, he was looking for a reason to lock me up. You could tell as much by the way he spoke to me. The questions he asked. He didn't believe my story, but I didn't care. I was sticking to it, and if he was a true mulatto, he'd allow me to do so. We gotta look out for each other.

I walked back inside and closed the door behind me. Moose was on the couch in his usual position. With Officer Hudgins gone, Moose was once again the center of my attention. My stomach sank a little. Was I really going to give him away? I had never considered myself the type of guy who would abandon his pet, but when keeping your pet may result in a prison sentence, I guess you change. For some reason I felt embarrassed. I kept imagining how I'd respond when people asked, "How's Moose? Or "Where's Moose?" Or "How come I haven't seen you and Moose for a while?" What would I say? I didn't have an answer. I couldn't decide which to be more ashamed of, the fact I gave away my dog, or my inability to man up and tell people I did so. They were both fairly "pussyish" in all honesty. I'll just tell people he died. That was a respectable, cowardly way out… and oddly…that didn't bother me.

TUESDAY 11:09 A.M.

I parked in the rear of Harrington's and sat in the car for a few moments. I wanted a little extra time with my possessions before I just gave them to someone else. Moose sat with his head out the window and sniffed the air. He was a handsome dog. His brindle coat was still shiny and healthy, even at his older age. I reached over and patted him on the back a few times. He half turned and looked at me but couldn't pull his full attention from sniffing the parking lot air. I grabbed the guitar from the backseat and sat it on my lap. Even though I seldom played it, I still was going to miss it. There's a freedom that comes with making music. Even if it's bad music, you can escape from the stress of your day and make something up on your own. Something that was 100% under your control. Where else in life do you get that opportunity? I think that's what drew me to the guitar in the first place; the opportunity to express myself artistically. That or the prospect of fame and loose women, it was certainly one of the two. What pulled me away from the guitar was my job and a lack of musical talent. Both were slowing down my progression.

I cracked the front windows and left Moose waiting in the car. With the guitar in hand, and a growing resentment for Mr. Rash, I slowly walked toward the staff entrance. I opened the door slowly and stuck my head inside. Only Andy was in the locker room. He looked at me and his eyes opened wide.

"What are you doing here?" he asked. "I'm supposed to call management the minute I see you."

"It's okay, Andy." I thought of my deal with Martha and said, "Besides, I'm going to stop by management on my way out. I promise." He stood still and I could tell he wasn't sure what to do. I turned to him and smiled before I spoke.

"It has been a pleasure working with you, Andy. I'm pretty sure you won't see me after today, so I just wanted you to know that, okay?" I held my hand out for him to shake. He walked over and grabbed my hand.

"Thanks," he said. "Is there anything I can do for you before you leave?" he asked. Seeing an opportunity to seize the moment, I calmly took Andy up on his offer.

"Actually, Andy, there is something you can do for me." I smiled and placed my hand on his shoulder. "You can wear those tube socks I gave you the other day. Wear 'em with all your might. That's what you can do for me." I patted his shoulder and turned to leave the locker room.

"Uhh...are you serious?" he asked.

"What?" I asked over my shoulder.

"Is that really what you want me to do for you? Wear those tube socks? 'Cause...I mean I can, but...it's not what I was expecting you to say. Kind of odd."

I stopped short of the door and turned back toward him. The room felt a little awkward. I scratched the side of my neck as I tried to explain my request.

"I was trying to leave you with something inspirational, you know? Like a funny story in the future."

Andy squinted and looked at the floor from the corners of his eyes.

"And you came up with tube socks?" he asked in a dumbfounded tone.

"Yeah, guess I missed the mark a little with that one, huh?"

"Yeah," he chuckled under his breath, "guess so." Neither of us said anything for a moment, and the awkwardness in the room grew. "So," Andy finally spoke, "I can wear the socks really. It's not a big deal. Just wasn't expecting…"

"Thanks, Andy. I appreciate that." I turned back to the door. "It's been great working with you!" I said walking out. "Take care, Andy." The door closed behind me, and I relaxed a little. Andy was a great guy, but I think that's why he made me so uncomfortable. He was *too* great of a guy. No one likes to see their own flaws on display and working with Andy did that to you. He even made me feel like a bad guy from time to time.

I headed for an elevator and scanned the first floor of Harrington's on the way. It was its usual busy self. The seniors on this floor were so different than the patients I dealt with on the second floor; hell, half of them looked like they could still beat me in a foot race. I stepped in the elevator and strummed the guitar a few times. When the doors opened to the second floor, I paused before exiting. This was it. I was really doing this. Goodbye guitar, goodbye job, and worst of all- goodbye Moose. The doors began to close and I stuck my foot out to stop them.

The second floor was its usual self; mellow and more depressing than the first. Be that as it may, I liked the second floor. I guess I had gotten used to it. Humans are impressive that way. The way we adapt to our environment. My first few days at Harrington's I was in awe at the sad living conditions these people had to tolerate, but after a week or two, I didn't feel that way any longer. I actually looked forward to coming to work. It was strange really. Over the years this dimly lit maze, full of coughing, hacking, and death stench had become a home to me. I enjoyed watching Mr. Rodriguez try to seduce Mrs. Rodriguez. It was fun. I liked talking with sweet old people like Mrs. Flockspart. And most of all, I loved bathing sexy old people like Mrs. Hawkins! Hell, in hindsight, even evening pill distribution was a good time. But all that was over.

I stepped out of the elevator and headed toward Mr. Rash's room. He was someone I definitely wasn't going to miss. In fact, if there was a silver lining to this whole mess, it was *not* having to see Mr. Rash again! I made my way to his room and avoided eye contact with people in the hall. I could tell people were surprised to see me. It was obvious word had spread about Mrs. Hawkins' death and my potential involvement. I found Mr. Rash's door partially open. I knocked lightly and entered his room. He was sitting in bed watching television. He smiled when he saw me, and I thought for a moment he might handle this event with some class. I quickly found out I was wrong.

"Well, well, well." He said while turning off the TV "I didn't think you'd have the nerve to actually show up." He smirked at me as he spoke. I could tell he was enjoying this.

"Whatever," I said. "Here's the guitar. So we're even now, right?" He took the guitar from me and plucked a few strings.

"Well I don't know if we're *even*, but you've kept up your end of the deal, if that's what you're asking. I don't think a guitar and murder even each other out if that's what…"

"I didn't murder anyone!" I interrupted. "You have no idea what you're talking about, Mr. Rash."

"Whoa, whoa. Calm down. I wasn't trying to upset you. The last thing I want to do is make you mad, okay?"

His words made me feel a little embarrassed, and I apologized for yelling at him.

"It's okay," he said. "I'm sure you're under a lot of pressure."

"Thanks, Mr. Rash, that's very understanding of you."

"Oh, I'm not trying to be understanding," he said.

"Then why'd you say it?" I asked.

"Because the last thing I want to do is make you mad enough to take me on a field trip and dump my body! I'm looking out for my best interests."

TUESDAY 11:38 A.M.

I left Mr. Rash's room and went to look for Martha. Before I left, he took a few more cheap shots at me and Mr. Corbit. Said he was happy I was leaving Harrington's, and he wished I would have finished off

Mr. Corbit like I did Mrs. Hawkins. To be honest, it took all my energy not to hit him. He was such a dick! Plus, I was forty years younger than him, so I was pretty sure I could kick his ass. It's wise to fight people that pose as little physical threat to you as possible, and Mr. Rash definitely fit into that category. However, he posed a major threat to me and my freedom, so I decided it best to walk away. But I was mad. I couldn't help but feel he was taking advantage of my situation. Not only was he basically stealing my guitar to show up another old geezer, he was also talking an unnecessary amount of shit while doing it. Everything about the man drove crazy. I left his room confident that if karma was a real thing, death would be approaching him soon. That would show him.

It was almost noon, so I knew Martha would be in the basement doing laundry. I popped my head in and called her name. She came around the corner and placed a sheet she was folding on a nearby counter. Before she could say anything, I told her to meet me in the parking lot and walked away. I wanted to get back to Moose. He had been waiting in the car and I felt bad about it.

Martha took her time coming out to the parking lot. That gave me a second to take Moose out of the car so he could stretch his legs a bit. He was excited. He whimpered and sniffed the air as if he was missing something both exciting and delicious inside Harrington's. It took so little to make him happy. That always amazed me; probably because I was seldom ever truly happy myself. Moose saw Martha approaching and began wagging his tail wildly.

"Well, well," she said, "looks like you kept up your end of the deal…for once." Perhaps I was still annoyed from Mr. Rash, but her comment upset me a little. I always kept up my end of a deal. As long as it was incredibly easy, I was incredibly reliable. Nonetheless, I responded to her inaccurate statement.

"Yes, I'm here," I said. "Looks like Moose is excited to see you." She knelt down and let Moose lick her face. She scratched his chest and spoke that annoying baby language people speak when petting dogs.

"Hey, big boy! I a scratch you belly, big boy. I scratchie watchie you belwy…" After about thirty seconds of ungodly baby talk, I couldn't take it anymore.

"So," I said, "you still wanna take my dog from me?" She quit scratching Moose's "bellie-wellie" and turned her attention back to me.

"I'm not taking your dog from you," she answered. "I'm taking you up on the therapeutic relationship you so kindly offered me earlier. It's your decision whether you give him to me or not. I'm not pressuring you one way or another." She smiled wryly and went back to petting Moose.

"Not pressuring me?" My voice rose with anger. "If I don't give him to you, you'll call the police and tell them I'm responsible for Mrs. Hawkins' death, won't you?"

"Absolutely," she said flatly.

"Do you have any idea how difficult this is for me?" I asked.

"Don't care," she responded. "You're not in a position to barter. Hell, you're not even supposed to be on company grounds." She stopped petting Moose again and looked me in the eyes. "You said your dog can help people, and I think you were right. In fact, I know you were right. For example, he can help you avoid jail time, and he can help me lead a more fulfilling life. So why don't you let him help us?"

I let Martha's words sink in. She had made some valid points, but one thing was still confusing. The way she spoke. I had never heard her talk like that. She was being both direct and rude. That wasn't like her. She was almost always direct, and I liked that about her, but she was never rude.

"I still have to stop by management and return my keys," I said. "They don't know I'm quitting."

"Yes, they do."

"What?"

"Yes, they do," she said. "Management doesn't expect, or even want you, to come back to work."

I was shocked.

"I mean think about it," she continued. "What kind of message would Harrington's be sending if they kept you on the payroll? And can you blame 'em? At the least you lost a resident which resulted in her death, and at the worst, you killed the resident yourself. I'm still undecided myself, but either way, you're not going back inside there. I'll take your keys in for you. I'll also take Moose."

And so it went. Within ten minutes of coming outside, Martha had taken my job, my dog, and a large portion of my pride. I guess women really are better at multitasking.

A couple of days had passed and things were getting back to normal, or as normal as they could be. I didn't care about losing my job. Even in a bad economy I could still find a job that underpaid and underappreciated me. That was easy. It was the other things that were bothering me. Just imagining Mr. Rash playing my guitar around the halls of Harrington's pissed me off. It's true I had all but stopped playing my guitar, but it was still my guitar. Able to be picked up and strummed anytime I felt like it. Now that wasn't true anymore. And the ironic thing was, with no job to occupy my time, I found myself wanting to play the guitar more than ever. Stupid, Mr. Rash!

But the job and guitar paled in comparison to Moose. I missed him. I mean, yeah, I never really took him out on walks, or did anything special with him, but I had grown accustomed to having him there when I returned home. By habit I kept waking up early to let him out for his morning sniff, spin, and shit in the backyard. But he wasn't there. He was with Martha now. I could see her sniffing, spinning and shitting with him. Until he left, I never noticed how attached to him I was. There was a silent feeling of responsibility with him in my life. I couldn't stay out too late because Moose needed access to the backyard. I couldn't leave town without boarding him or having someone house sit. Now I could stay out late or leave town anytime I wanted, but this new sense of freedom didn't make me happy. I missed him relying on me for his two meals a day. Now no one relied on me. My days now consisted of trolling for ass at the gym and smoking the weed in my cereal box. It was like being in high school again, except I didn't feel cool. I was lonely.

I made numerous calls to Rachel and Amanda, but they weren't answering. It didn't surprise me that Amanda was avoiding me, but it wasn't like Rachel to ignore my calls. She would usually call me back and see what I wanted, but now it was as if she didn't even care. Someone who did seem to care about me was Officer Hudgins. He called or came by at least once a day. I avoided him like the plague. When he called, I let it go to voicemail. When he stopped by, I laid motionless on the floor. Needless to say, he wasn't the company I was looking for, but at the same time it was nice to know someone was thinking about me.

Looking at the clock, I saw it was closing in on one in the afternoon, so I decided it time to hit the gym. Since it was a nice day out, I thought walking to the gym would be a good idea. I went to the fridge and grabbed the cereal box off the top. I still had a large amount of weed left. Smoking a joint or three a day doesn't put much of a dent in an ounce. So I rolled another one and grabbed my gym bag. After locking the door behind me, I was on my way. It was sunny, and cool, but not cold. After I had walked a hundred yards or so from my house, I lit the joint up. Something about smoking in public made me feel like a rebel. If you saw me from your house, you'd think it was a cigarette, but if you walked by me, you'd know it was no cigarette. I think it was that sneakiness that made me feel like a renegade. Looking like I'm following society's rules, but in actuality, I'm just giving it the middle finger.

FRIDAY 1:22 P.M.

What was normally a six-minute drive to the gym took about a half hour to walk. I had finished the joint some time ago now and was fully stoned now. Combine the high with the twenty minutes left on my walk, and you had the prime ingredients for mind wondering. I began to think about everything that had happened the last week. My life was irreversibly different. I couldn't help but blame Sean for everything. If he hadn't stolen Rachel from me, I never would have taken Mrs. Hawkins to the park. If Mrs. Hawkins never went to the park, she'd still be alive today, I'd still have a job, I'd still have my guitar, and most importantly, I'd still have Moose. It was obvious Sean was responsible for all my troubles, but I learned none of that mattered. Life didn't work that way. It was up to me to make the best of the awful position Sean had put me in. Maybe it was the fresh air on the walk, but I was beginning to see the potential positives of my situation. Sure, I had lost almost everything I valued in my life, but I wasn't the only one suffering. This mess was affecting everyone negatively. Martha was desperate enough to look to my dog for inspiration. Amanda was obviously using sex to compensate for a lack of self-respect (I mean why else would she have slept with Toucan?). Rachel was lonely enough to believe Sean was more of a man than I was. And Toucan? Well, Toucan was crazy. He was so crazy the police wouldn't even believe his murder confession. It doesn't get much crazier than that. So in the big picture of things, I wasn't doing so badly. My new life was going to take some adjusting to, but I'd live. I didn't know if I could say the same for them.

That's why I started going to the gym every day. Since Rachel and Amanda were out of my life, I needed to find a replacement. Therefore, I started lifting weights for the same reason all men lift weights; to pull skirt. A better outer image increases your odds of finding someone to ignore your inner flaws. That's just science. Basic animal kingdom shit, really.

Now my gym was typical. It had three types or groups of patrons that frequented it. The first group was the muscle heads.

These were the men or women who stayed at the gym for hours. They lifted, talked, and carried bottles of water or protein shakes. They were there when I got to the gym, and they stayed well after I left. The interesting thing to me was how less attractive these people became. The guys became so big they just looked uncomfortable, and the women…well, they didn't look like women anymore. I don't know a man that wants a woman with shredded six pack abs and veins in their arms. Or a woman that can lift more than he can. That is not attractive. It's creepy.

The second group or type of person who goes to the gym is your average Joe or Jane. Ten pounds overweight, exercises after work, can't stop eating sweets, and therefore, never really sees any progress. I definitely fit into this group. While our intentions are good, we never seem to make the jump to that first group I described. We get overwhelmed with work or family or whatever. So we stay ten pounds too heavy and dread summer swimming attire. It's frustrating, but at least we're not part of the next group.

The third group of people who go to the gym were actually a tapestry of individuals. They consisted of old has-beens, obese lazy-asses, or makeup- wearing floozies looking for a new boyfriend. These are the people the previous two groups mock and judge. The muscle heads ogle floozies, and the average Joes pad their egos by comparing themselves to the fat and old people. I found the whole scene eerily similar to a nude beach; full of people comparing, judging, and overcompensating.

Nonetheless, once I finally arrived at the gym, I went to the dressing room to change. Then I stopped and looked at myself in a mirror. I was curious if I looked as high as I felt. In short, I did. My eyes were bloodshot and droopy. But I didn't care. I was there to work out, not win a sober looking contest.

The main floor, which held the free weights, was crowded and noisy. It was much quieter upstairs with the cardio equipment. So upstairs I went. I preferred to work up a sweat before I started lifting weights. Made me feel like I was burning more calories that way. Also, if I lifted weights first, I knew I wouldn't do any cardio. I'd just get tired and go home. Treadmills aren't the most exciting machines at the gym, but they were the most effective in cutting weight. I needed to lose ten pounds and working out upstairs was the best way to do it. Another bonus to using the treadmill or Stairmaster was the abundance of women on the neighboring equipment, and today was no different. Thirty minutes flew by as I watched the toned ass of a young Asian girl in front of me. She was around 24 years-old, thick, and by the look of her gray spandex shorts, wasn't wearing any underwear. A patch of sweat was beginning to show at the small of her back. I stayed on the treadmill another five minutes just to watch the sweat spread to the crack of her round ass. My legs were burning at this point, but as I watched her cheeks lift and drop, left to right, I knew I made the right decision.

The rest of my workout was rather uneventful. I did some bench press, curls, and some abs. Your basic vanity muscles. Who cares how strong you truly are as long as your abs, arms, and chest are ripped? Those are the muscles women care about, so those are the muscles I focus on. Whatever would help me find the next woman. I was going to need help getting over Amanda...whom I was using to get over Rachel. There was a system to the rebound.

With a quick scan of the gym floor I looked for any single, available-looking women. Seeing none, I decided it time to hit the sauna. I loved to sit and sweat in saunas or steam rooms. It was one of the few things I classified as thoroughly relaxing. Outside of avoiding eye contact or petty conversations, there was nothing I disliked about being in a sauna. They gave me time to think, and on this day, in this sauna, I thought about Moose. I thought about Rachel and Amanda, and Mrs. Hawkins. Basically, I thought about everyone I had gotten involved in this mess. They all had different places in my life, but I was fairly confident they all cared about me, and as a result I began to feel something new. I felt sorry for them.

For twenty minutes, I sat in that sauna and slowly pieced everything together. It was complicated, but I began to understand everything that had happened in the last week plus. There was no doubt I had lost a lot- my dog, my guitar, my job, and my wife, but it could have been worse. Yes, Martha asked a high price for her silence, but she gave me her silence all the same. The same could be said for Mr. Rash, Toucan, or Amanda. These people could make my life hell or even put me in prison, but they weren't doing that. Why? Because they care about me. Rachel may have been ignoring me at the moment, and, yes, Amanda was trying to conceal our sexual encounters, but they still cared about me. If they didn't, Sarah and Drew wouldn't be sitting in jail for a crime I inadvertently committed. I smiled and relaxed a few more minutes before finally leaving the sauna. I couldn't help but think everything was going to work out in the end.

FRIDAY 2:34 P.M.

After changing back into my street clothes, I slung my gym bag across my shoulders and headed out of the gym. The air was cool, but it became much more comfortable as my walk progressed. About six blocks from the gym I started to become hungry and changed course to grab a bite to eat. There was a wing joint around the corner that sold shitty Chinese food, but wonderful wings. I wanted to get an order of teriyaki wings with blue cheese. What better way to treat your body after working it out? I rounded the corner and saw the restaurant on the next block. As I crossed the street, I saw a couple walking a dog coming in my direction. The people were too far away to make out, but the dog sure looked familiar. He was big, tall and brindle. It was Moose. I stopped walking and waited for the couple at the corner. Once they were a hundred feet away, they seemed to recognize me, and I began to recognize them. I just didn't understand why they were together. It was Martha and Toucan. I didn't know they knew each other. Martha said something in Toucan's ear and gave him Moose's leash. Moose saw me, or caught my scent, and started to run towards me. Toucan pulled on his leash but Moose drug him reluctantly along. I met them halfway and petted Moose vigorously. He was happy to see me and that made me feel great. I was happy to see him, but I was confused as to why he was with these two.

"What the hell is going on here?" I asked. "What are you up to, Toucan?"

"I'm not up to anything, bro" he responded in shock. "I'm only doing…"

"Let me explain everything before you start to flip out," Martha interrupted.

I continued to pet Moose and looked back and forth between the two of them. "How do you two even know each other?" I asked. "And why are you bringing my dog into all of this?"

"First of all, he's my dog now," Martha said forcefully, "and second, we were on our way to see you, so if you relax, we'll explain everything, okay?"

"Go ahead," I exclaimed. "You have my full attention."

Martha took a deep breath before she began to speak. "Like I said," she began, "Russell and I were on our way to your house."

"Wait a minute," I interrupted, "your name's Russell, Toucan?" Toucan seemed embarrassed.

"It's my birth name," he responded, "but most people…"

"Toucan is something he will not be answering to anymore, right, Russell?" Toucan nodded silently and avoided eye contact with both of us.

I was amazed at what I was seeing. I knew Toucan was a bit on the "crazy" side, but even for him this was strange. He continued to look at the ground.

"Why is Toucan acting so weird?" I asked. "Is everything okay?"

Everything's fine," Martha responded. "But let me ask you a question."

"What's that?" I asked suspiciously.

"How bout you let me buy you a drink?"

FRIDAY 3:09 P.M.

After I agreed to the drink, "Russell," Martha, and Moose walked me halfway home. On the walk, Martha told me how she and Toucan met. According to her, she was taking Moose for a walk after work one day, and as she was strolling through the skate park, Toucan, or

"Russell," came out of nowhere calling Moose's name. She stopped, he petted Moose, and the rest just kind of happened. They both swore their happiness together and thanked Moose for it. She told me I was right about Moose and the happiness he could bring to people. Toucan mimicked her sentiment while adding the deep insight of, "He's a special dog," whenever Martha allowed him to speak. I was more than skeptical of their story. It hadn't even been a week. How could these two form such a deep bond in that short of time? How could Moose change someone's life that quickly? It seemed to me they were laying it on a little thick. I doubted the sincerity of their story. But then again, if anyone was capable of these accelerated emotions, it would be someone as crazy as Toucan and as lonely as Martha. Anything was possible with these two lowlives.

Before we separated, they told me to meet them at Lumpy's in a half hour for the drink Martha had promised me. I think they were afraid to take Moose back to my house. He probably wouldn't have left with them if he saw his old house again. They knew this was his real home.

I went inside the house and grabbed some water from the fridge. Without Moose, my home routine was considerably different. There was no one to let out to use the restroom. No one to feed. No responsibilities outside myself. While these things should have made me happy, they didn't. I became jealous that these concerns were now Martha's and not mine. I missed Moose and seeing him a second ago didn't help any. I threw my gym bag in the laundry and headed for the stash hidden in the cereal box. When I took out the bag of weed, I quickly remembered why Martha now had Moose and why I was stupid to miss him. "Freedom tastes better than dog kisses," I told myself. It was right to give him up, but it would take time to stop missing him. I rolled another joint and looked at the clock. I needed to meet Martha and Toucan at Lumpy's. Before I smoked, I made a turkey sandwich and ate it while watching TV.

Why did Martha want to buy me a drink? Hadn't she told me the whole story about her and Toucan on the walk home? What else did she need to tell me? Or was this her way of saying thank you? Buy me a drink, thank me for Moose, and go our separate ways? It made sense. Martha was pretty rude to me before I left Harrington's, so an alcohol sponsored apology seemed more than reasonable.

After I finished the sandwich, I sparked the joint and set out on my way to Lumpy's. Smoking while I drove, or walked, or sat at home, had become the norm for me. With no job and no dog, my life had become more and more like a college kid's. A perpetual haze of weed smoke and physical activities. While that lifestyle was quite satisfying at 22 years old, it was oddly unfulfilling now.

FRIDAY 3:41 P.M.

I pulled up to Lumpy's and took one last drag off the joint. With more than enough left at home, I flicked it out the window and reached for the bottle of clear eyes in my glove box. With my eyes white, and my mind right, I went inside ready to accept Martha's beer-soaked apology. I felt good. I mean things hadn't worked out the way I had envisioned, but at least I was going to get a little recognition for something.

From the looks of the parking lot, Lumpy's was empty. Just the local drunks at the bar at this time of day. I locked the car and headed inside. The good vibe I had upon entering the bar was erased when I opened the door to see Garrett bartending. Did he ever get a day off? Feeling the urge to take the high road, I mustered up a smile to greet Garrett with, but it proved worthless.

"Hey, douchebag, your friends are waiting for you at a table in the back room." I said nothing in response, only glared at him. Apparently, Garrett was not taking the high road this afternoon. I made a mental note to flip him off on my way out of the bar.

The back room of Lumpy's was a place I seldom went. There was nothing in there but a few tables and some dart boards. Before Lumpy's was Lumpy's, I think the building used to be a steakhouse. So I guess the back room was an extra dining section or something. But that was years ago. Now it was nothing more than a smokey room used primarily for storage. Why Martha wanted to meet in there was beyond me. Perhaps she felt more comfortable thanking me in private?

I stepped in the back room and was quite shocked by what I saw. Not only was there a table full of people I knew waiting for me, but Moose was there too. I stood holding the door open as I took in the scene.

"Hey, bro, thanks for coming," said Toucan as he walked toward me.

I turned around and yelled, "I thought you couldn't bring dogs in here, Garrett?"

"I don't have a problem with dogs," he responded, "just some of their owners." He chuckled and smirked at me from behind the bar.

"Goddamnit I hate him!" I said softly under my breath. By this point Toucan was leading me to the table. He pulled out a chair and asked me to sit in it. I did so. Across from me there sat Toucan, Martha, Amanda, Rachel, Sean, and Officer Hudgins. It was a who's who of my social network. "Why's he here?" I asked pointing at Officer Hudgins.

"They asked me to come," he responded. "Said they might need my help."

"Need your help? With what?"

"With this exitvention," answered Martha.

"What the hell is an exitvention?" I asked. The answer was simple. An exitvention is quite similar to an intervention: an organized, or team effort, designed to get a desired action from another individual. In this particular case that individual was me. And what was the action they wanted from me?

"We want you get wost!" Rachel said emphatically.

I was stunned and unsure what to say. Just an hour ago I thought these people cared for me. Now, assuming "wost" meant "lost," they were telling me to leave them alone. How could I have misjudged them so severely? I looked at Rachel. She was sitting next to Sean. Amanda was on the other side of him. Figuring now was my last chance to win her back, I asked Rachel the things that were on my mind.

"So you don't love me anymore, Rachel? Not even a little bit?"

"Pease! I never wuv you," she said. "Our marriage strictwee bidness."

Sean chuckled and placed his arm over Rachel's shoulder. He looked at me with a pompous smirk. "Looks like she's moved on," he said. "Why make this any harder than it has to be?" He smiled again and squeezed Rachel tightly with his arm.

"So the point of this exitvention," Martha continued, "is to set up boundaries that..."

"Hold on a second, Martha. Are you serious, Rachel? This is honestly the guy you want?"

Before she could respond, Sean cut in, "She already told you, asshole! She wants me. And you know what? She ain't the only one that wants to ride the Sean train!"

"First of all, didn't I already kick your midget ass for talking smart to me? And second of all, no one wants to ride the "Sean train" as you put it. You're a loser. And the generic title of your love train proves it!"

"Really? Well if all that's true answer me this: Why is Amanda a passenger on my train?" He placed his other arm around Amanda's shoulders and squeezed both her and Rachel tightly. I sat still and let what I just heard sink in. Sean had now taken my wife and the woman I was using to get over her. Simply put, he was dominating me. I used the only comeback I had.

"What's the problem, Sean, can't find a woman of your own? Gotta steal my leftovers?" Even as I said it, I knew the words rang hollow. It was a weak attempt to hide my frustration. So weak in fact Sean merely laughed in response. He knew he had won that battle. I slumped in my chair to lick my wounds. After a moment, I looked up at Amanda and asked, "Why?"

"I'm sorry," she said. "I wasn't trying to hurt you, it just kind of happened."

"It just happened, Amanda? You just happened to end up sleeping with my wife and her boyfriend? How in the hell does that just happen?"

"Maybe we should focus on the exitvention?" Martha interrupted.

"Actually," Amanda said with a smile, "I want to answer his question." With lavish and sometimes graphic details, Amanda explained how she and Rachel and Sean became an item. To summarize, it turns out the vans at Harrington's are insured by Sean's insurance company, and after my firing, Harrington's needed someone to go down to the insurance company and explain the whole Mrs. Hawkins dying thing, and the van's role in her death. Long story short, she saw Rachel, liked her outfit, one thing led to another, and they had a threesome in Sean's office.

"You screwed him in his office?"

"Actually, she screwed us in my office, bro. The Sean train makes many stops, my man." Amanda shot him a glare and he stopped talking.

"I thought you said you weren't a lesbian.

"I'm not a lesbian, you idiot. I also had sex with Sean. A lesbian wouldn't do that."

"But a whore would!" I interjected. "A whore would have sex with me, Toucan, and Sean, and that's exactly what you've done! The only person you haven't slept with here is officer Hudgins." A silence fell over the table as everyone looked at Officer Hudgins.

"That's correct," he said, "I have not slept with her."

"Thank God," I said.

"However, Amanda," Officer Hudgins continued, "my shift does end in a little over an hour, so if you're free, I'd love to get to know you better."

Amanda smiled. "That sounds fun," she said. "Do you have to leave the handcuffs at the station or can you take 'em home with you?"

Officer Hudgins grinned coyly, "The cuffs go whenever I go. You never know when you might need them."

"Enough! What the hell is going on here?" My outburst earned everyone's attention at the table. Before anyone began to speak, I seized the moment and aired my internal monologue. "Seriously, somebody explain what is happening here! Martha's with Toucan, Rachel never loved me, and Amanda's about to be bound and stuffed by the officer at the end of the table…does that about cover everything?"

The table was silent for a moment. Then Sean cleared his throat. "Um…actually…you forgot the part about Amanda riding the Sean train. That's an important fact. You might wanna…"

"If I hear one more thing about the fucking Sean train, I'm coming over the table!"

"Oh, really?"

"Yeah, really!"

"Well in that case…"

"Well in that case nothing!" Martha cut in. "Both of you morons shut up! We're not here to hear about who's having sex with who. And besides, who cares? We've all had sex with Amanda, so what? The reason you're..."

"Wait, Martha, wait. You're not implying that you've had sex with Amanda, too, are you? Because I think we all know that didn't happen, right?" Martha looked at me with an irritated expression. Amanda looked embarrassed and down at the floor. "Oh come on! Martha, too?"

"Look," Martha said, "none of that matters now. We brought you here today for a reason. An exitvention. All of these people here have taken time out of their schedules to ask you to leave them alone. To exit their lives. Can you do that for us?" The whole table was looking at me now. No one said a word. I started to feel uncomfortable. They were seriously waiting for a response to her question.

"So you guys want me to leave you alone? Like, what do you mean "alone" and "exit" your lives? What does that even mean?"

Martha sighed and clasped her hands together in front of her. "It means to cease all contact and communication with everyone at this table for the remainder of your natural life. Do you understand?"

My embarrassment was growing. I was being disowned. I felt the back of my neck becoming warm and began to fidget in my seat. "Well what if I don't want to leave you guys alone? What if I decide to just hang around and bother you?"

"You don't want to do that," Officer Hudgins broke in. "For starters, that's harassment. And secondly, I'd hate to have to reopen the investigation into Mrs. Hawkins' death. Be a shame to find out the wrong people are behind bars for that crime, wouldn't it?" He said nothing more and stared at me with flat eyes. I suddenly realized he knew everything. And that meant everyone at the table probably knew everything, too. I was stuck. They had successfully boxed me in. From behind me I heard Martha repeat her question, "So whatta ya say? You willing to exit our lives?"

THURSDAY 12:52 P.M.

It took almost two weeks before the finality of the exitvention truly hit me, and when it did, I didn't know how to feel. I mean, it's not every day your wife, coworkers, and acquaintances come together to shun you. Needless to say, it's a sobering experience. I dealt with it by getting intoxicated. Frequently. However, after a couple days of drinking, I decided to put the booze down. I needed to clear my mind. Bryant Park had a track built around its perimeter, and with Drew and Sarah in prison, I started running there to lose weight and clear my head. And the thought that kept running through my head was that I had been defeated. I had called all the shots, made all the moves, and I had lost. There was honestly no one else responsible for my life at the moment. I had made my mess, and now I was forced to clean it up. Why are the simple things in life the most difficult to accept?

After returning from the park, I threw my sweaty clothes in the hamper and took a shower. The hot water cleansed my skin, but it did nothing to calm my mind. Everything kept replaying itself in my thoughts. I tried to think about other things, but one recurring thought continued to eat at me. It was that I was the only one suffering. In fact, only *my* life had taken a turn for the worse. It was me who lost my job, lost my wife, and gave up my dog. Meanwhile, everyone else had a new love interest, a new pet, or a new guitar to play with. It was my sadness that was improving everyone else's fortunes. It stung to come to that realization, and I decided to do something about it.

I stepped out of the shower and walked back to my bedroom. As usual, and for my neighbors' entertainment, I stood naked in front of the window and put my clothes on slowly. Fully dressed, I decided it time to sit down and figure out a plan of action. I had cut back on my drinking, but my smoking was only increasing. I felt it helped me de-stress and focus, and this was one such occasion where I wanted to do both. The weed I stole from Drew and Sarah was still in a cereal box on top of my fridge, and I had already smoked nearly half of the ounce. I put a Sublime CD in the stereo and rolled a joint at the kitchen table. My mind slowed and I began to concentrate on how to put the embarrassment of Mrs. Hawkins' death, and the fallout thereafter behind me.

In order to truly move on, I was going to need to make a few changes to my physical and mental being. For starters, I had to forget about Rachel, Martha and the rest of them. I had to remind myself that they were all douchebags at heart, and I shouldn't mourn their absence in my life. True, the way they all teamed up to exile me did hurt, but what was I really losing? In fact, upon further inspection, this cast of minions actually hurt me more than they helped me. For example, Rachel was nothing more than a trampy opportunist. She had left me for someone she perceived as better, and I was sure she'd eventually do the same to Sean. Toucan was a brain-fried loser who needed meds to be even close to sane. Martha was a rugged, stubborn woman shaped like a fridge and so socially inept she chose to spend the majority of her workday alone folding laundry. Not a real people person. And Amanda? She was merely a pro-bono prostitute that I mistakenly thought valued her body and who she gave it to. But I was very wrong. She put no more stock in sex than she did shaking hands. They were one in the same to her. Which made her essentially a walking venereal disease. Why would I miss any of these people? I took another hit off the joint and told myself that as cliché as it was, perhaps this was actually a blessing in disguise. I could take advantage of this opportunity and become a better person because of it. And not only that, but I could also surround myself with better people. Increase my chances of moving up the social ladder.

Feeling a sense of motivation I decided on a few basic changes. Changes that could improve me. I inhaled another toke from the joint and imagined an improved me. What would that look like? For starters, it would involve me not drinking before noon. To quit drinking entirely seemed unrealistic and unnecessary. However, I had to admit that unless in college, being drunk before lunch is completely inappropriate, and that no responsible adult would partake in such behavior. It's about success. And simply put, it's hard to be successful if you're slamming beers or taking shots at 10am.

Change number two: rededicate myself to physical fitness. I would hit the gym with a newfound ferocity. Not only would working out improve my health, but it would also improve my confidence and make me more attractive. To put it bluntly; a better outer image makes others more willing to ignore your inner flaws. That's why a hot girl, no matter how crazy she is, is always in a relationship. His friends tell him to leave her crazy ass, but they don't know how good she looks naked. Therefore, he ignores his friends' advice and tries to work it out one more time. Women will claim they're different, but they aren't. They'll say it's more than a man's appearance that matters to them, but a muscular guy always has a woman waiting at home for him. Fat guys come home to cats, roommates or moms. It's just the laws of science.

The last, and perhaps most important change, was something I had already tried to do- become more like Moose. This whole mess started with me attempting to behave in a more "Mooselike" manner, but obviously, I had failed miserably. As I admitted this to myself, I felt a tinge of embarrassment in my stomach, but it was short lived. Perhaps it was the weed, or perhaps I had learned something from all of the recent drama? Whatever the case, what had become apparent to me was that I didn't need to be embarrassed. Sure Mrs. Hawkins was dead. And, yes, I may have had something to do with her death (that was certainly debatable), but the important thing was I could learn from my mistakes. Tomorrow could be a better day, and I could be a better person. If I let it bother me that Drew and Sarah were being punished for a crime they didn't commit, I would be living in the past, and I couldn't do that. Moose didn't live in the past. He lived exclusively in the present. So while I did feel bad for Drew and Sarah, my framing them was in the past and there was nothing I could do to change it. Life goes on, and you've got to move on with it. I put the joint out and packed a bag for the gym. My new life started now. Drink less, work out more, and live in the moment; those were my three rules. If I followed those simple instructions, I would be a new me, I would be an improved me, and I would be a happier me. What other motivation was needed?

THURSDAY 1:33 P.M.

I left the house and headed to the gym. I drove the long way. Like a heartbroken lover, I wanted to drive by Harrington's. Just to look at it. See if anything had changed. I did the same with my ex-girlfriend's house in high school. There's something in male DNA that makes us gluttons for punishment. Harrington's looked normal. Nothing new. As I passed, I imagined Mr. Rash inside with my guitar, and that made me mad. But then I pictured Martha with Moose, and that made me sad.

By the time I got to the gym, it was packed. Finding a parking spot is a lot like looking for the friend you lost at a concert- too hard to find and always in the one spot you didn't look. This day was no exception. I finally found a spot in the next to last row. The walk was longer than I would have liked, but that was okay; I would use it as my warmup. "I'm working on the new me," I reminded myself.

The inspiration from my new perspective enhanced my workout performance. I lifted hard, I ran hard, and I sweated hard. When my stomach began to burn from sit-ups, I called it a day. To relax afterwards, I decided to go to the steam room. When I got to the locker room, I noticed I hadn't brought a towel with me. I hadn't brought hardly anything with me. I must have been really high when I left home because all I packed in my gym bag was a hand towel, socks, and a water bottle. While this sucked and highlighted why I needed to quit smoking, it was really an inconvenience at most. I'd wear my shorts in the steam room, then grab my bag, throw on my shirt and shoes, and run to the car. I was parked so far in the back that exiting out the back door was faster anyway. Feeling satisfied with my plan, I shoved my clothes in a locker and headed for the steam room.

This was my first time using the amenities at my gym. Actually, it was my first time in the entire pool area. I was surprised to find that the steam room and sauna were open to both genders. I was suddenly glad I had decided to wear my shorts. Au-natural probably wouldn't have gone over too well. There were three people in the steam room counting myself. One was a woman, white, brown hair, small, round breasts, and in her early thirties. She had an innocent face, but guilty eyes and it made you wonder which was lying. I saw she was married, so I paid no more attention to her. The other inhabitant of the steam room was a man, white, brown hair, slightly balding, slightly overweight, and in his early forties. He looked like he loved baseball, drove a minivan, and always voted Republican. We all sat in silence and stared at various areas of the steam room. A couple minutes passed before the girl started up a conversation with the other guy in the room. They talked about, -what else?- how hot it was in the room. This went on for a few moments before I joined in the conversation. Four minutes later and I learned she was from Florida originally, so she loved the steam room or sauna. They reminded her of home. "Hot and humid," she said.

About the other guy, I had learned he and his wife vacationed in Florida often. They, his wife and he, were big fans of cruises. "They're great," he said. "You need to check one out soon." After saying this he stood up, wished us both a nice day, and left the steam room.

It was silent and a little awkward after his departure. In an effort to break the ice I said, "Well, he was a nice guy."

"He was," she echoed. "I've never been on a cruise either."

"Yeah, never made my list of things to do," I said. "But then again, I'm not the best at making lists."

"What do you mean?" she asked.

"Well, take today for example. I forgot to bring a towel with me." I laughed and shook my head. "Little things like that always seem to slip my mind."

"I totally know what you mean," she said. I'm the same way…" She then went on and told me numerous examples of her forgetting to turn off things like the oven or unplugging things like her curling iron. She was nice. I made a concerted effort to avoid looking at her chest or making any sexual comments. This was the new me. Somehow our conversation came back to her growing up in Florida, except this time she went on to explain her getting married and moving. She asked if I was married or had children. I told her I didn't have any kids and I was in the process of getting divorced. She told me she was sorry to hear that and said something about her husband and kids, but, honestly, I wasn't listening. I was hot.

Feeling proud of myself for not hitting on her and wanting to get out of there before I fainted, I stood up and said, "It's been great talking to you, but I'm getting a little dizzy, so I think I better get out of here." I opened the door to the steam room and stepped out in a bit of a hurry. The air outside of the steam room was extremely refreshing, even though it smelled like chlorine. I put my hands on my head and breathed in as much air as I could and waited for my head to stop spinning. As I was about to gather myself to leave, the steam room door opened and the woman from inside came out.

"Everything alright?" she asked.

"Yes, I'm fine. Thank you. I just got a little too hot, that's all."

"You sure you're okay?"

Yeah, I'm good. Thanks." After I said this, she didn't walk away or start to leave. Instead, she stood, fidgeted and smiled coyly.

"What are you going to do about a towel?" she asked?

"Oh yeah, I'll just grab my stuff and run out the back door. I'm not parked far."

"Or you can just dry off at my place."

The words came as a complete shock. I froze up. Did I hear her correctly, or was my brain still broiled from the steam room? "I'm sorry, what did you say?"

"I said you can dry off at my place if you want." She smiled and looked at me with her sultry eyes.

"Aren't you married?" I asked while stealing a peek at her chest.

"Yeah, but I told you my husband and kids are out of town. Don't you remember?"

"Oh is that what you said? I was getting so hot in there I couldn't hear straight. So your husband's out of town, huh?"

"Kids, too," she responded.

We looked at each other, awkwardly, for what felt like entirely too long. It was obvious she was waiting for my response and wasn't going anywhere until she got it.

THURSDAY 2:57 P.M.

I felt good on my walk back to the car. I knew I had made the right decision. It wasn't easy, but perhaps I really was changing? The last time I picked a woman up at the gym, I ended up going back to her house, stinking up her bathroom and getting into a fight with her boyfriend. Not one of my shining moments. So when presented with a similar opportunity, I knew what I had to do. Only an idiot repeats the same action and expects a different outcome, Einstein said that, or something close to that. The point is I didn't need to be Einstein to know what was right. I told her thanks, but no thanks. And then I walked away. It was weird. She watched me walk away as if waiting for me to turn back and change my mind, but the weird thing was I knew I wasn't going to turn around.

The light breeze in the parking lot seemed extra chilly in my wet shorts. I broke into a light jog and hurried to the car. Once inside, I put the heater on low and started the engine. But before I backed out, I looked at myself in the mirror. It was an odd feeling, and it sounds stupid to say, but I was proud of myself. I turned down guaranteed sex from a very attractive woman. And why? Because Moose wouldn't have done it, that's why. If Moose were a human, he would have said, "Sleeping with a married woman is only going to bring you, her, or someone else trouble." And he'd be right. Because when you're honest with yourself, nothing good comes out of infidelity, excluding the sex. I backed out of my parking spot and headed for the exit. This may have been a small event to anyone else, but it was huge to me. The old me would have taken that woman up on her offer in a heartbeat. No questions asked. But not the new me. The new me had grown.

On the drive home, I couldn't shake the feeling that I deserved a reward of some sorts. A little something to show myself how proud I was...of myself. Since the weed had worn off, I was inevitably hungry, so ice cream was my first choice. But after I had eaten a medium sugar cone of mint chocolate chip, I still felt I deserved something. Something bigger, but I didn't know exactly what it was. I drove around downtown for twenty minutes. I took roads into parts of town I had never seen before, but nothing struck my fancy. I didn't want food, I didn't want clothes; none of those screamed, "Good job!" or, "Way to go!" Maybe ice cream really was the best I could do. Since I had no idea where I was, I decided it wise to go back home. I turned right onto a skinny street that ran behind a series of buildings. I had never noticed this street before. It was a dead end and easy to miss from the main road. There was a liquor store on the corner and a few shady looking businesses behind it. I went to turn around in the liquor store parking lot, but something, perhaps the same voice I had listened to at the gym, convinced me to turn around at the dead end instead. As I came back up the street, I suddenly saw why the voice in my head had told me to keep driving. It was leading me to my reward.

I parked the car and looked at myself in the mirror once more. "Change comes in degrees," I said to myself. I had done well today, but I would fail in the future. "And that's part of life," I said looking at my reflection. "It takes time to truly change, and only you can be the judge of your change. Martha and Rachel, and all those other assholes think they got the better of you. But guess what? You're changing, big guy. You're gonna be better tomorrow than you are today. Don't get down on yourself. Moose wouldn't do that. Now get in there and get your damn reward!" And with that I got out of my car, smiled and locked the doors. I smiled because I knew I was right. I did deserve a reward, or better yet, a happy ending. Change is hard. What wasn't hard was my decision to lock the car doors. Ju Ju's Magic Hands Massage parlor was in a bad neighborhood. Better safe than sorry.